BORDERLINE

An Oral History of The Brexit Wars 2020 - 2022

Declan Daly

(Non Fiction)

Medevac: Flying The Irish Air Corps HEMS Mission

The Waiting Men

May 2020

OP 4A: (Near the border.)

Heartrate 102. The pair had just arrived in between the gorse bushes, off to the left of the thicket as viewed from the target and with three other , more obvious, locations to hide between them and the man they came to see. The crawl into position denoted effort and this was reflected in the beats per minute on the Corporal's wrist. It would come down as he controlled his breathing. They were settling in now, the sniper and spotter were camouflaged, ahead of time and securely out of sight of prying eyes. Stillness, now, and self control were the name of the game. Rather than shrug his shoulders in a normal fashion to relax and potentially make an observable movement, he rolled them down and around to the front in a circle. Tilting his head to the right slightly, he looked down along his nose to the left at the other man sharing their small hide. The spotter, ten years senior to his twenty six, already had his scope, which resembled a stubby telescope on a short tripod, up on their objective and was lying immobile. The sniper made a comparatively large motion to lift the stock of his bolt action rifle and brought his cheek down to it, allowing his right eye to look through the sights at the small farm house four hundred metres to the front of their observation post and here his focus would stay for the remainder of the job.

The clouds drifted lazily in the summer sky, a light breeze blew left to right across his arc of fire and somewhere nearby a bird, having become quickly accustomed to their presence, was chirping again.He took in his sports watch with a quick glance.

61 beats per minute. Getting down to resting heartrate.

Wolf 3 - The Left Seat: (Casement Aerodrome, Baldonnel)

Sitting in the left seat of the AW139 helicopter, the co-pilot was wondering if it could reasonably be considered murder if, under the present extenuating circumstances, he killed the man next to him. They had briefed to death for this job , waited for the notice to move for days and now they were here, pre-start checks completed, troops on board, ready to light up the engines and go. Anyone could, or should, under the circumstances act as if something of moderate interest was happening. Admittedly they'd been put on five minutes notice to move over an hour ago. Yes, they had done everything they could do prior to putting the fuel pumps 'on' and the engine switches to 'flight' . But his colleague just sat there, dark visor down on his helmet, which was itself tilted back to lie on the headrest of the right seat. Seventeen minutes ago he began to absently smack his lips. The wet pop was barely audible with his own helmet on, but he could see it. It shouldn't bother him, but it really did. Enough to contemplate whether a lethal response was acceptable.

"Do you want the prestarts again?" In other words, please do something else with your stupid lips except smack them.

"Neg dude, they're all done, just chill and wait for now I suppose"

" Yeah, just in case we missed anything, you know?. If i keep him talking he can't smack his lips!

"They're all checked and checked again, let's not mess around too much or we will move something we shouldn't. Be a shame to blow the floats or something by accident at this stage."

With that , the man seemd to lie further back in the seat if that was possible, crossed his hands over his body armour and behind the visor, there was almost no doubt his eyes were closed.

"Gotcha" (Not much else to say to that).

He looked past the apparently understimulated pilot at the

other helicopters which were lined up waiting like themselves., then over his right shoulder at the rest of the crew. The crewman had his feet up on the stretcher, the medic was digging around in his daysack before triumphantly pulling out a Mars bar, which he offered to no one. They would only get called in if something bad happened with the Garda insertion teams on the other helis. Maybe the adrenaline wasn't required after all. Right now anyway. The crewman gave him a silent thumbs up, not even raising his hand off his thigh doing it. He returned the gesture in an equally lacklustre fashion and turned back to the front and exhaled. He shuffled in the seat again.
Pop.
It had started again.

OP 4A:

Heartrate 48. It had been a quiet night. The target had gone to bed around eleven, or at least the lights had gone out and movement in the house had stopped. They had long since recce'd the building from their position and all the admin in the field tasks associated with the Observation Post (OP) were complete. They just had to watch and then act in accordance with the brief. They had started the daytime routine again - no movement and back on optical sights after a night of looking at the green glow of night vision equipment. Settling his body he always found easy, get comfortable, breath in, hold, breath out , wait for the carbon dioxide build up to tell your brain to repeat. It was a steady, rhythmic and a reliable way he had found, to not move for long periods of time. To keep his mind focused on the job he had other tricks. It was easy when all that could be done was done, to daydream and get distracted. To counter this, he would look around the target again for some innocuous detail. Last night he noted that open ends of barn on the left hand side of the yard had rusted to a lessor degree than the sides. This morning he was observing that the paint on the pebble dashed wall of the gable end of the house could do with a lick of paint.

3

The expected visitors probably wouldn't notice, but flecks of gray were appearing under the white surface. Starting to look a bit weather beaten like their owner. Speaking of which, the sun was now up. If the occupant of the house stayed in bed much longer, he'd miss half the day.

Wolf 3 – The Left Seat:

He would ask for something from the right door. The flight manual maybe. As the other pilot leaned over he would use the Heckler and Koch 9mm pistol in his chest rig , base of the skull and bang. Job done. It would be difficult to get the gun out and cocked before anyone reacted of course and shooting small arms in confined spaces , where everyone else was also armed, was always going to have certain fatal drawbacks, but ultimately it would be worth it.

The move from idle consideration of the legal defence he might mount, to actively planning to commit acts of violence, had been triggered by the addition of tongue clicking half an hour ago.

Three clicks in a row followed by one exagerated smack , pause for three seconds and begin the cycle again. And again.

OP 4A:

Heartbeat 60. He could hear the helicopters in the distance. Dull and muffled by the rolling terrain close to the border but there none the less. The man they came to see was outside now and apparently heard them too, looking to the South. Certainly greyer than some of the photos in his file, his hearing still worked. Broad shoulders but with less meat on his frame now, it was still easy to see how he had once cut a more impressive figure. One to be feared. One to be removed, when the time came.

Wolf 3 – The Left Seat:

Listening in on the VHF radios, not much was heard except the odd series of clicks and uncustomary quiet. The lip smacking from the other seat had stopped when they got the word to go (a very low tech thumbs up from an Air Corps HQ officer standing in the Air-Traffic-Control (ATC) tower with a landline beside him). Thirty five minutes later, they were hanging back in a holding pattern at altitude while the other two helicopters in their flight did their thing. Standing off at this distance, he couldn't see them but from the array of briefings he knew that some certain event had occured that led to an Emergency Response Unit team from An Garda Siochana being launched to intercept a car and its' occupants. Violence was expected. Medevac may be required. So here they were. Looking over his shoulder, the crewman and the medic had lost the look of affected boredom they had on the ground and replaced it with a look of readiness. In the front right seat, the occupant was leaning further forward in his straps with a tight set jaw. Their was little chat – prearranged codewords over their secure frequency would be the next instruction they would hear, with very different implications. Rampart: Medevac required, Landing Zone (LZ) secure. Darkline: Medevac required, LZ not secure. Seminar: Mission successful, return to base.

Minutes passed like decades. The radio clicked once and then a voice, slightly higher and tenser than normal.... 'Seminar'. That was that. Unburned adrenaline, left him wondering if this was a good or a bad result, but at least they had gotten airborne. They dropped height and waited for the other aircraft. Once they arrived at the designated rendezvous, they would return to Baldonnel as a loose formation. There was really little to do now.

OP 4A:

Heartbeat 52. The man they came to see continued looking to the South for a good minute after the noise of the aircraft had faded. By the look on his face, he had been waiting for them to come closer, to approach, to land. Maybe he had been waiting for the people in the intercepted car which had been stopped well out of sight, but he couldn't have been expecting them, the passengers in the car with their own lethal intent. Maybe it was a legacy of a violent life that you half expected it always? He went inside through the back door, closing it behind him. The Corporal couldn't see him but felt sure he was on the phone to someone. Knowing what that was about would be another units job. The codeword that had come through indicated that the three armed personnel in the car had been stopped and detained without shots fired. The drama was over for the overt units for now, but for them it would be several more days of waiting and watching. He rolled his shoulders down and to the front.

Comdt Brian Raferty, AC – Retired (Wolf 3 – Left Seat)

'It was later, not long before he died actually, that the bastard told me he was doing that lip smacking thing on purpose. He could see that everyone was wound up and knew annoying me would at least make the others feel a bit more experienced and ready to go. I suppose fresh co-pilots make an easy foil that way. He was telling me this when I was on my command upgrade course, which by that stage was as much on the job training as a formal course of instruction. We were short enough of bodies at that stage that you just got the training done when you could which wasn't really ideal, not the way we used to do it.

Anyway, we were doing the usual sitting by the campfire thing in the mess in Finner Base one weekend on duty and got chatting about when we each thought it had all really started, you know? Some said the Brexit Referendum, some said when the journalist, Lyra McKee was killed, that the eh, the various groups wouldn't have had the political confidence to do that before. But the consensus was that em, that for us in the Air Corps, or in No 3 Ops Wing anyway, we only found out about the other stuff going on later, that for us it all started that day. That was when things went from the occasional real job to routine internal security ops and on and on from there.'

Pauses (approx 10 seconds)

' You know I still miss that fecker. After everything and every other death that came after, you know the way some people just stand out when they go? It was as much about eh, you know, he was senior to me at the time, obviously, but he was always the first guy I'd go looking for to go for coffee. Always good for a chat and keen to pass on what he knew rather than guarding it. Funny fucker and a good pilot with it. SAMS don't care about that though.'

Sgt Dan Morris (Corporal on OP 4A, RIP)

'We'd been give a pretty good brief on what to expect, I mean , if those lads had driven through the interception point or anything like that, we were going to be the last point that they couldn't get past but things would've been fairly gone to shit at that stage. We were told that it was basically a house cleaning exercise by dissidents prior to a new campaign and that they were out to take out a number of old Provos who would still have held some sway in the area before they could operate there freely. It was considered bad for the peace process if they succeeded. Stopping them with weapons on them, but before they got there was the name of the game but we were there I suppose number one, as a last gasp effort to stop them and number two to watch what happened afterwards, who came to visit that kind of thing. Jesus, if I'd known how long I'd spend crawling around those hills I'd probably have been a lot less precious about my heartrate!'

Introduction

The opportunity to observe history as it happens is rarely afforded historians. The chance to record the lived experience of those involved, to chart their own views as they change with time and as a result of what they see and do is rarer still. The conflict over the last few years in Ireland, which has become known as the Brexit Wars, offered one such experience. The current cessation in violence may or may not be permanent, but with a sense of optimisim that could equally just be a weariness of hurt, now feels like it is a good time to give the viewpoint of some of the personnel of the Irish Defence Forces who served during this time. Their voices add colour to the official histories and in some cases, their continuity from the start of military operations joins the dots on what can otherwise become seperate major events that reach the public eye against a background noise of lower intensity operations.

This account comes at a time when tensions have reached a crescendo, where an internal security operation for Ireland developed into external operations involving the EU as a political bloc and France and the UK as individual countries, along with the, as ever alleged, support from Russia; who armed both sides in the sectarian fighting in Northern Ireland. These tensions have begun to ebb as everyone realises how close to a conventional shooting war they really came. Hopefully, they will fade to nothing, or very close to it and the internally and externally displaced people can begin to go home. It is also important to recognise that this is an account from one perspective only, that of the members of the different military branches of the Defence Forces. It is freely acknowledged that this perpsective cannot represent a whole war nor does it attempt to. The majority of this book consists of material drawn from interviews conducted by the author and others as part of the DF Oral History project, the aim of which is to record the experiences of DF members on an ongoing basis. As the events of recent years are so fresh and so close to home, some contributors have asked not to be identified by name, nor even to have their complete interviews used in an anonymous manner. In some cases, the contributors cannot be named because of the work they conducted during their service (it is unlikely that members of the Army Ranger Wing (ARW), Explosives Ordnance Disposal (EOD) or the unit known as The Red Team will be openly putting pen to paper any time soon). Where this is relevant, the author has used their accounts, or combined several accounts to form a narrative that gives a deeper context to events.

CHAPTER 1

*Status Quo, More or Less – The
background to an emerging war*

**Senator (Formerly Brig Gen) Ian Davis, Minister for Defence ,
Retired**

' *The lead up to the war had begun sometime before we ourselves
realised it had actually commenced. It of course originated from the
manner in which the Brexit negotiations were progressing, I suppose
one could say it had already commenced from about summer of 2020
against the backdrop of ongoing Covid-19 related issues which, eh,
the distraction of which, provided cover for an expansion of IRA activity along the border area .*

*As we later discovered, arms shipments from Russia to the IRA had
already commenced at that time. Whether they had chosen the IRA as
a prototype for their future actions later on, or whether they actually
considered that this was the vehicle through which they were going
to exercise their policy is still unknown. What is known, is that during this time the IRA had begun to actively recruit again - they had
received substantial weapons shipments from Russia, some training
was provided, but they did not have the bodies to use that information or equipment effectively.*

What became clear very quickly, however, was that the IRA intended to make use of this newfound largesse and, presumably working on the lines that nothing succeeds like success, they would need to carry out some operations in order to recruit new blood into the organisation. It's important to point out at this stage that the IRA did not exist in the same way as it had throughout the 70s, 80s ,90s and into the 2000s. It was very much an organisation that existed on paper there were some command elements left, some control elements left, but it was an organisation that did not have foot soldiers anymore. In that regard it could not be expected to carry out any campaign, but it needed to do something in order to draw those foot soldiers in from a community that realistically wanted nothing to do with another campaign of violence. Throughout the whole war as we've seen it, no part of the community in Northern Ireland actually wanted another conflict; all of it was driven and supported from outside.

As Customs and Border vacancies began to be filled in the docks and in the airports in Belfast, from where much of the trade would make its way between Ireland and Britain , the IRA found their first targets - customs officials, border officials, these people were hit up quite early on. They were obvious targets, of course, the PSNI had tried to protect them but you can't be everywhere at once. The IRA attempt here was obviously too encourage a new revolution, as they saw it, but that was for external consumption – really they needed to assert themselves in the border area where they were already being squeezed by the PSNI and other armed groups. They saw early on that that - something that everyone realised as time went on - that while the border between the EU and Britain might exist in the sea, in reality anything going through that border was always going to have to travel overland via the existing border between Ireland and Northern Ireland. Papers might be exchanged at ports, but for everything else, the border was at the juncture of the UK and the EU on the ground. That was critical – that was where the different legal and political systems actually rubbed up against each other and the resulting friction was there to be exploited by those who would seek to 'fundraise' for their groups by smuggling etc and by those who would seek to put their arms and people out of reach in another jurisdiction.

Controlling the area around that border was something that the IRA had to do in order to exist, never mind run their campaign. And it was always something that was going to be contested, not only by us, but also by the other players who emerged into the sectarian violence the terrorist milieu that then was spawned once again in Northern Ireland. This was simply because, the group that controlled access to the land border, de facto controlled the illegal movement of people, arms and the off books trade between the UK and the EU. The emerging groups challenged each other as a result for access, to deny the others access and crucially to recruit people as footsoldiers.

This issue of recruitment was a critical one for the survival of each group. Due to the means of their genesis, they did not have the ability to continue growing or replacing losses organically like might have happened in the old days. There was a finite number of people from all communities who were willing to involve themselves in violence at any given time; as I've already said, the community support wasn't there. The result, especially for the Republican sides, the Unionist side quickly became more homogenous, was that whoever was winning gained the most recruits but there was never more than about one thousand total throughout the whole war from either of the two main traditions in the North.

What also became clear very quickly and for a number of reasons was that Britain was not going to put a large force of troops back into Northern Ireland. It was very, very, much realised that to kind of re-launch an Operation Banner 2 for example, would play exactly into the arms of the IRA and other Republican movements and would be the best recruitment poster they could hope for. In addition, one only has to look at the Tory party polls at the time, and in the lead up to 2020, where it was quite clear that the majority of the membership of the Tory party would sacrifice Northern Ireland as a part of the UK in a heartbeat, in order to protect their vision of Brexit . This, more so than perhaps any other factor, this laid the ground for what happened thereafter as it gave the groups on each side time to get through their labour pains and become established and organised.

As the PSNI struggled to contain this new and emerging IRA threat, obviously other threats began to appear. The resurgent Unionist groups, and also other Republican elements began to emerge suddenly being very highly funded and very highly resourced in terms of modern weaponry and equipment. The PSNI was being backfilled not by troops in the main, obviously specialist EOD units and Special Forces (SF) and Intelligence(Int) elements etc were in position in Northern Ireland, but generally speaking they were backfilled by ordinary police from elsewhere in the UK, from Britain itself. These police were not only unhappy to be there themselves; they also became the first targets for the resurgent Republican groups especially the factions in Belfast and the other urban areas away from the border.

It became clear quickly that the IRA was still attempting to utilize some of its old ways of operating, in that it would use cross border tactics, that some of the weaponry and personnel it was attempting to draw upon were to be based in the Republic as opposed to Northern Ireland . This is because basically, the geographical position of the remaining command structure that existed at the time, ex-Provisionals were mostly living along the border area and in some cases controlling the criminal enterprises along that border area. The upshot of this is the view amongst Republicans that the Republic might be a safe area ,mistaken as it was, and this led to control of the border being heavily contested amongst Republican groups who sought to make use of the jurisdictional differences between not only Ireland and Northern Ireland but between the EU and the UK. This basically became the first phase of the war.

From our perspective, the Government and the Defence Forces were absolutely not willing to allow terrorists forces to operate from our territory and utilising such assets as we did have on hand at that time - and it must be remembered that the Defence Forces was already in a state of crisis in terms of its personnel issues - the military contested control of the border and in large part succeeded quite quickly . The speed at which we succeeded, notwithstanding some of the darker elements of the Black Winter, was a major success which is sometimes overlooked now given the events which followed. Did we succumb to hubris in the aftermath of what appeared to be success? If we did, we did not have long to be humbled.

Our policy at the time and one which I enforced by dealing directly with the Chief of Staff to a greater degree than previous ministers was based on one pretty essential fact that must be grasped. Recruitment on its own was not solving the ongoing shedding of personnel within the Defence Forces and that retention of experience also had to be one of the key goals. The whole personnel issue was a major point of mine, which we addressed in a number of different ways. One of these of course, perhaps most famously, was the massive reintroduction of reserve units more in the model of the FCA rather than the newer Army Reserve template. In addition, we brought in an active reserve into both the Air Corps and into the Naval Service, to take advantage of the amount of people who were saying they wanted to still contribute. These were ex-personnel who wanted to still contribute, but who felt that a full-time career back in the Defence forces was still not going to work for them.

In addition of course, we had the massive drive to recruit new blood into the regular Army, the regular Air Corps and the regular Naval Service. This of course is the lifeblood of the Defence Forces as it is the core component. It was from the Permanent Defence Forces that greater than 90% of our overseas commitment still came, the decision having been made early on to maintain our overseas commitment, that there would be no repeat of the withdrawal from Cyprus to fix domestic problems. Overseas was seen by the Govt as one of the essential roles of the Defence Forces, indeed it was the jewel in the crown of the foreign policy of the country in many ways. it must be said that others would talk about foreign direct investment as one of the foreign policy great successes, however, it was during the Black Winter when foreign investors started to ask about security - physical and cyber security, for their companies that we really started to see both the Dept of Foreign Affairs and crucially the Departments Finance and Public Expenditure and Reform really pay attention to properly funding and resourcing the Defence Forces.

I mentioned that the Defence Forces were the jewel in the crown of foreign policy. Well if the Defence Forces are a diamond, recruitment is mining for coal. If you want to turn coal into a diamond you need two things, you need time and pressure. Time is time, you can't change that. Pressure comes from experience be it overseas or domestic and we used the newfound interest of the finance and public expenditure officials to insure that the troops that we already had were financially able to stay in the DF without crippling the future of their families. In that regard we faced many challenges at the start, especially as we intended to grow our numbers as quickly as we could, but we absolutely needed to keep enough of our old school of Non-Commissioned Officers (NCO's) and Officers in place to teach the new forces we were building. This was critical because the position of the Defence forces was not well matched to the threat posed by the IRA and the other groups that contested the border region at the outset of the Black Winter. We needed to create time for ourselves to polish the diamond, to allow our personnel, our organisation, to grow in experience while also denying that opportunity to the enemy.

The policy that we adopted in taking on this task was that a doctrinaire approach would not work, that simply adhering to the notion that you need ten regular troops to defeat one guerrilla or one terrorist, was not something that we could do from the start. Some have looked at the activities we took on and said that we were throwing things at the wall to see what stuck, that's not true, we looked at the challenges that the IRA were also facing, that the various terrorist groups were facing and sought to create operational problems that they couldn't solve. We sought to throw more scenarios at them in their planning stages than they could deal with and ultimately that worked, at that stage of the fight and with that particular opponent.

What this involved, in the end, was simultaneously running a num-

ber of programs - obviously we had the Starforts of the Black Winter,
we had the treating the border area as an overseas trip and rotating as
many regular troops as we could, while reinforcing and replacing
them with the new reserves. We introduced the small unit warfare approach, using the *reserve troops for patrolling, patrolling,*
patrolling. Keeping that constant pressure on and then ultimately we
introduced the combined warfare element as well, using naval forces
ultimately proved successful not only for patrolling but also in a fire
support capacity in the Cooley Peninsula area and also the constant
ISR (Intelligence, surveillance and reconnaissance) presence of the
Air Corps in addition to other more obvious roles such as fire support
and transport, parachuting and logistics etc .

Indeed, some have specifically noted to use of airborne troops and
clearing out certain areas such as the Sliabh Bloom mountains as
vanity projects, or as justifying expenditure in certain areas. None of
that is true. It was all part of a deliberate policy, a deliberate process,
of introducing so many different variables that no terrorist group
would have the capability to plan and defeat them all simultaneously
or to prepare to defeat them all simultaneously. Using the example
of the airborne troops, once we had used them initially in the Sliabh
Blooms, intelligence did report that assets and personnel were being
diverted by the IRA and by everyone else to cover likely drop zones in
advance of planning any operation. This in its own way was a suc-
cess as well ,in that it diverted people away from carrying out aggres-
sive action against the State.

That is not to say of course, that any of this was easy or without cost.
The ultimate kind of cost.'

I have left Senator Davis's account about the start of the war
intact and unedited as it brings to the fore some of the speaking
points that inevitably come up when people ask 'why?'. Why
did the Russians get involved? Why did our neutrality not protect us? Why did the Defence Forces and the Gardai not lock
down the border immediately? Why did the PSNI not use their

resources to tackle things North of the border and the crucial question in regards to this phase of the war : Even if they were now flush with weapons and money, why did the remains of the Provisional IRA return to violence, when the GFA provided a roadmap to lasting peace and when talk of a border poll on a united Ireland was having to be addressed by multiple political parties in the Republic?

Answers to some of these questions are straight forward, others challenge long believed narratives in modern Irish culture. In short order, as these issues have been covered at length both generally in the press and specifically in academia and other books, the Russians were already involved. Following the Cold War and more specifically the wars in Chechnya and Georgia, the Russians had developed and honed a method of warfare or subversive activity that combined information warfare through social media and state run news agencies, traditional cyber warfare through hacking of personal accounts to develop *Kompromat* – compromising material used to coerce a person to do their bidding – and moving up through these levels to fostering armed groups of insurrectionists in a target country.

These activities generally proceeded in a manner that was, if not invisible, non-attributable to any state actor and sometimes remained entirely covert. Once the time arose to move out of the shadows, the armed groups would be sometimes joined by unmarked Russian forces and certainly would be accompanied by Russian advisors. This multi spectrum warfare was seen to greatest effect in the seizure of the Crimean Peninsula and the move into the Donbass region of Ukraine. The ground was prepared through information warfare and the military action was presented as a *fait accompli*. There was no military option available to other nations to undo what had been done. Russian interests were advanced at the cost of another country and that was that.

In talking about how they targeted Northern Ireland, it must be remembered that they were already suspected of having influenced the Brexit campaign, through all the methods mentioned short of use of force. With the Brexit campaign successful from their point of view, they had achieved something worthwhile – they had separated a significant state from the heart of the EU project. They may have hoped that taking out such a main player would have led to the collapse of the EU itself, but the manner in which Brexit played out in public probably put many Euro sceptic parties off the idea as the ramifications became obvious. Nevertheless, it was a victory in and of itself that the UK would leave the EU.

Then the world was struck by the coronavirus pandemic. The world suffered, Europe suffered, Russia suffered, and the UK suffered. It is now believed, that Russian policy was that, in order to hold position economically and politically on the world stage and perhaps even advance itself further, the campaign against Western Europe should be moved to a new level. By distracting Europe and damaging it, Russia would have a freer hand in the 'near abroad', the area that Russia believed fell under its own sphere of influence in eastern Europe and elsewhere. By distracting and potentially damaging the integrity of the UK, it could prevent it from emerging as a competing player in the event of a best-case scenario Brexit. Northern Ireland presented itself as a two for the price of one deal in this assessment.

With existing sectarian history to ignite, Russia began a directed online campaign, targeting those people who could be used by them to best affect, *Kompromat* was used to silence those who could best oppose those voices at a social level. In choosing to arm the IRA, it seems now, - but may never be confirmed – that they were chosen because they already had a residual command structure in place, even if they had no remaining paramilitary force to speak of. Simply put, they represented the quickest way of starting an armed conflict in Northern Ireland. This activity obviously soaked up the attention of the security services and obscured the fact that men and women of fighting age were disappearing for months at a time before reappearing and leading very different lives.

Such a return to conflict of course affected the Republic of Ireland. 'But we're neutral' was often the refrain when the extent of outside interference in our domestic affairs became known. In response, I can do little better than quote Comdt Dave Heally when I asked him about the general public discussion he encountered as a member of the DF:

'People would say 'but we're neutral' as if this meant anything, as if simply professing neutrality was a shield that would ward off all aggression. And it was infuriating to try and say this over and over again; that you had obligations if you're neutral that, you know, just saying it wasn't enough you had to back it up by providing security and people just wouldn't get it, would not get it at all . If you look back in time towards, say, when Lemass for example was saying that we had no problem with joining NATO, the only problem at the time was obviously that, at that time, we had contested ownership of Northern Ireland, but people forgot that or just didn't know.

Neutrality, or the perception of neutrality, had become such a revered institution in Irish culture and mentality that people just never questioned whether it would actually work. Whether or not you would have to update the way you approached the whole subject, but people just couldn't grasp it, could not grasp that this wasn't some eternal thing that would shine a light and shoo off all darkness.

The best analogy that would work with most people, that I could eventually think of, was the 'Sleep when the baby sleeps' analogy. What this was, I just compared it to when you have a new baby in the house and especially if you've got a couple of kids already and you're exhausted, you're fatigued, you've just gone back to work people are saying 'how you're going?' and you go 'I'm tired' and , some well-meaning soul, they'll say 'just sleep when the baby sleeps' . As if nothing else needs to be done in the house, as if this glorious little notion of sunlit information, hadn't penetrated the sleep deprived depths of exhaustion that you're suffering through, and you know then; straight away; that nothing you say to this person will work. That you're just so completely in different places in terms of the life experience that you're going through and most new parents can relate to that. And that's what I would say to people: 'but we're neutral' is the 'sleep when the baby sleeps' of the whole Defence discussion. If that's where you are, you're so far behind the ball that you're just never going to catch up to where things are now, not without listening to the experts in the field. Neutrality wasn't going to ward off anything and it certainly wasn't going to ward off the intentions of a country that just saw starting an insurrection and violence as something that would protect its own interests elsewhere.'

Neutrality then, was not a shield. But why did the Gardai, who were responsible for internal security, and the Defence Forces not lock down the border as soon as violence broke out.? The answer is unfortunately simple – it would never have been possible. People almost always cast their minds back to the era of the Troubles when they ask this. They forget that both organisations had shrunk dramatically since then. The Defence Forces of the 80s had an establishment of 14,500. The same organisation at the onset of violence was understrength and under resourced and far short of its promised establishment of 9,500. It resembled more the army of 1969 in terms of resourcing and numbers than the one that was eventually cut to pieces in various cost saving efforts and 'peace dividends.'

Add to this that the reorganisation of 2012 cut away the border barracks and battalions in order to preserve core units and that various specialties within the DF were critically understaffed – Air Corps Captains, the people who filled out many of the operational rosters in that service, were at 62% of establishment in

August 2020 for example – and you found an organisation that was already under significant stress just to tread water, before having to tackle the extra requirements of a war at home.

Gardai were faring little better. Against a promise to put an extra 200 hundred new gardai into border regions in the early part of 2020, in fact Gardai were being sent from the college in Templemore before they had finished training, purely to deal with the coronavirus pandemic all over the country. The administrative backlog this created, as well as a reduction in the experience levels of a force based on community policing, cannot be overstated. Dealing with all of this absorbed the capacity of the various HQs just as much, if not more, than operational issues.

By simply not having the manpower, and no way to magically produce trained personnel, a total lockdown of the border, a check every vehicle, stop every hiker effort was just not possible. The counter to this is that from this poisoned acorn, something great did emerge but it all took time. Time in which the existing personnel would have to hold the line such as they could.

As to why the IRA chose a return to violence. Simply by having weapons, they became a target for the other republican groups who had remained active over the years as a source of weapons and eventually the new Northern groups as well. These groups and the PSNI began to squeeze the border based IRA from the North at the same time as Gardai and the DF began to squeeze them from the South. Having been monitored so much for the preceding twenty years, their membership was well known, and they needed new cells for security reasons, for operations and in order to control the border area. Recruitment meant having to be relevant in a world where sectarian tensions were being stoked from abroad via social media. Relevance meant violence. Deterring enemies meant violence. Control meant violence.

In the shadow world they existed in, simply living meant having to show your teeth and this they did. Early notions that some of their membership could sustain the peace process if protected were swiftly abandoned once it became clear that they were intrinsically involved in the resurgence of pain that was happening throughout both Northern Ireland and Ireland itself. It was at this point that the Black Winter really began.

CHAP 2

The Black Winter

April 2021. Lieutenant (Lt) Brian Quinlan looked over his shoulder at the woman still asleep with her back to him in bed. As arguments go, last nights was up there with the best he'd seen and he reckoned it might be the last one. He got it, of course, none of it was easy for anyone but giving him shit about being away all the time was a bit much when, as a cabin crewmember on the ongoing PPE runs around the world, she wasn't around too much either. And there was a war on. And he was in the Army. He felt like a lot of leeway should be kind of implicit in that. They were both over tired from work, on the second bottle of wine (still half drunk on the table, last he saw) and things had gone downhill again. Either way, it was time to go.

He wondered if they hadn't been in lockdown together last year and if her apartment hadn't been a ten minute walk from the Brugha would they have been together this long at all. Convenience vs increasing mutual distaste for each other? Such philsophical wanderings aside, he began the process of getting out of bed. What hurt today? Old favourites , his lower back while he was still lying down for one. He shuffled to the edge of the bed and swung his legs out slowly. Standing up, his right ankle felt like someone had poured dry rice krispies into the joint and his left knee nearly went from under him with the sharp pain that was now more or less normal when ever he put any kind of lateral load on it.

Half waddling, half limping with one hand on his warm, spongey feeling, painful lower back region, he snap, crackle and popped his way to the bathroom with his remaining lower joints joining the dawn chorus of complaint at being made to move. This, he reminded himself for the millionth time ,is not how twenty five year olds were meant to get up. But, landing badly after a overly enthusiastic ' hey looked the Lt jumped before the hover' dismount from a AW139 near the border in December had had a lasting effect on him especially since resting in any way was out of the question.

In the bathroom he surveyed the shelf at the window until he saw what he wanted. She always seemed to have a stock of painkillers in here somewhere, the good ones that you couldn't get in the chemists but which she stocked up on in passing through airports. He'd miss those. He popped two of the amber liquid filled capsules in his mouth and, considering his upcoming departure forever, decided to throw the rest of the sheet from the box into his shaving bag. A hot shower (and strong, not available over the counter, levels of codeine) sorted out the worst of the pain issues for the moment and he was a bit more positively disposed to the world when he left the bathroom. From the bedroom door, he took one more look at the still sleeping figure under the duvet. Should he wake her? Say something? No, enough had been said last night. Grabbing his bag from the hall and closing the front door behind him he put on his sunglasses, face mask and earphones. Backs. Knees. Relationships.The Black Winter had really fucked a lot of things up.

The period beginning in October 2020 and running until the end of the March 2021 has entered the public lexicon as The Black Winter. A number of events compounded each other to seriously dent the country's morale and put doubt on it's ability to cope with further stressors. This of course made enemies bolder and our own forces were put under even more pressure. The re- emergence of the IRA as a heavily armed threat surprised many commentators as the Russian connection had not yet been confirmed publicly. The change in tactics away from the old *Green Book* of IRA doctrine should have been less of a surprise than it was. Half a century old and put together under different circumstances, it could only be expected to have changed. Internationally, the relationship between the UK and the EU, but particularily Ireland, was becoming more charged as the full implications of Brexit began to bite down.

Perhaps the greatest driver of national stress though was the failure of the first Covid-19-19 vaccine to provide protection to the majority of the community. Peaking at 35% effectiveness with 18 – 35 year olds and with a low of only 11% for the over 65 groups, the rush to market had resulted in an imperfect product. These numbers too, only reflected the healthy, fit individuals that could take it. Those with underlying conditions were often precluded due to to some of the side effects which, while temporary, could exacerbate problems for those with breathing and cardiac issues already. The disappointment of this product coincided with the series of localised lockdowns and restrictions that had to be reintroduced to deal with Covid-19 flare ups in some parts of the country. These would be a contentious and continuous feature of The Black Winter with serious economic and human impacts.

Also around this time came the start of the second wave of deaths from the first wave of infection. Many of those in the younger age groups, who were presumed to have fully recovered began, from 5 – 9 months post Covid-19 recovery, to suffer from strokes and cardiac events. This was especially the case for those involved in physical work or sport and usually involved a sudden onset of symptoms. Over the course of The Black Winter, one hundred an eighty four people between the ages of eighteen and forty died of Covid-19 related strokes and heart attacks, with another six hundred and two surviving with mixed levels of recovery.

Thirty four of these people were members of the Defence Forces with eleven of these dying. For an increasingly small organisation, these were big numbers, especially as most of them occured in Cavan. As the location accounting for seven of the fatalaties , the Forward Operating Base (FOB) in Co Cavan known as Starfort 4 was considered a cursed location before it eventually burned down. As there were also four combat related deaths and a stunning twenty four injuries in and around the base, it was little surprise that no one in the Defence Forces was sorry to see it go.

◆ ◆ ◆

The short life and slow death of Starfort 4

A snap and admittedly temporary move to put troops back onto the border, the Starforts were a series of earthern embankment and HESCO container constructions designed to house and support a Company (Coy) strength unit in the field. In practice there was rarely more than a Platoon plus, around fifty people. Compared to similar FOBS such as the one used in Goz Beida in Chad, the footprint had shrunk significantly, there was no real empty spaces and the only clear area of any considerable size was the flat area left open as the helipad. The walls were folded in towards the centre to allow mutual support from the observation posts at each corner and to channel any potential attack into a kill zone between them. Viewed from above, they resembled a four pointed star, hence Starfort. The line of FOBS were not numbered in order East to West, but in order of construction – Starfort 11 for example was the next position East of Starfort 4. They were never comfortable but Starfort 4 was considered the worst of all for a number of reasons.

The first was location. Whereas the other FOBs were mostly located on highground, or at very least a tactically sound location, Starfort 4 was nestled at the bottom of a small wooded ridge which lay to the North and with smaller sets of hills East and West. Rumours were that the fields on the highground belonged to the relative of a TD and were removed from the list of compulsory purchase orders. This left the FOB not only in an unenviable tactical position, but also built on what was essentially a miniature flood plain for the river that flowed around the area in a semi circle to their South. This meant that the ground was almost always wet, and in a FOB where that ground was constantly churned by feet and wheels, that meant omnipresent mud. According to the troops who passed through it, the only relief from the mud in your sleeping bag came when the ground froze during Winter into spikes of sharp dirt instead.

The next problem for Starfort 4 was it's role. Whereas Starfort 1 for example, near Dundalk sat on a hill looking over the M1 motorway, essentially functioning as an especially grand OP, Starfort 4 was a patrol base. The surrounding terrain meant that was very often foot patrols. The soldiers assigned to it went out each day and night in the Winter conditions to come back wet and cold and sleep in the muddy portacabins which sat inside earthern revetments. Most agreed that just existing there was hard enough before the first Covid-19 19 deaths in early December 2020, hot on the heels of the first two combat deaths due to mortar fire in November which were the third and fourth fatalities of the war for the Defence Forces.. The account below is based on interviews with Cpl Diane Keane whose mother served in Starfort 4.

Company Sergant (CS) Valerie Keane was a tough woman. A head taller than most of the soldiers she oversaw, the forty seven year old Cork woman had joined the Army in 1992 serving two trips in Lebanon in the early and mid nineties, another in Kosovo and one more in Syria in 2014. The last one had been the hardest, only because her daughter Diane was now old enough to understand what was actually going on when 'Mam went to work for a longtime'. She had spent most of her time as a fitter having done an apprenticeship after recruit training, servicing vehicles but when the opportunity for promotion to Company Sergeant meant a change back into her in-fantry clothes, it hadn't bothered her. Not much did. Working on the premise that if you're going to be in charge, be in charge, those working around her quickly picked up on a few key points. Always have your act together, be on time and she was always 'CS'. Not 'Valerie', not 'Roy' a recruit nickname based on her surname, temperment and Cork roots - 'CS'. And you should probably be standing at something like attention when you say it.

Right now though it was back to her days in the workshop that her mind took her. She remembered a moment when the LTAVs (Light Tactical Armoured Vehicles) were brand new. A rep from the manu-facturer was excitedly showing her pictures on an iPad of an oil sam-ple they had sent them from a gear box on a broken down vehicle. The sample showed tiny sharp fragments of gear coating in precise detail much to the pride of the rep. He seemed less concerned that the gear-boxes were eating themselves and the then Sergeant (Sgt) Keane had voiced her displeasure pointing out that they knew from the clogged filters and black sludge coming out of them that the machines were 'pieces of shit that might as well have had cinder blocks instead of wheels because they never fucking moved'.

But that image of the oil sample, mysteriously plucked from her head from many years ago, summed up how she felt now. Her lungs were coated with hot oil run through with tiny fragments of razor sharp metal. Her heart was an engine revving itself to death trying to keep her lungs pumping in and out in search of unattainable oxygen. Every atom in her body felt like it was on fire and her vision was already tunneled. Sitting on the muddy camp bed outside the female shower block that served as a bench, she knew already what she had, she'd seen plenty with it here by now. But she was the CS, and that made the next bit harder even if the only extra thing to hurt was her pride.

The ambulance was only twenty metres away, sinking into the mud in the centre of the FOB. It was here to collect Private (Pte) Damien

Morris, a big, cheeky young lad from Limerick who had come back from a morning patrol taken his helmet off complaining of a sudden severe headache and promptly collapsed, with loss of all movement on his left side. At that stage she'd only had a bit worse of a cough than yesterday. Three hours later though (the weather was apparently too bad for medevac by heli) and the ambulance might as well have been a marathon away. She'd better move quick all the same, she could see the crew were getting ready to move (she half grinned internally at what was going to happen when they tried to spin off in that mud with those road tyres). With as deep a breath as she could take in – an ineffectual one at that – she rocked back and then forward onto her shaky feet.

She felt like she was wading through tar to move herself towards the paramedics, who seemed less busy than they had. This registered but the sheer effort of walking stopped her working out why. One was inside and the other about to head to the cab to drive when she grabbed the back door for support. In between deeply laboured pants she spat out " I think I should come too." The two medics looked at her and then the strectcher where her eyes followed. Pte Morris was still laid out, she could see his eyes wide open, one pupil blown fully dilated, the other a pinprick. He didn't blink and didn't move. "Yeah, we'll make room, we can come back for him later.' It sounded cold coming from the paramedic changing his gloves in the back , but it was delivered as sympathetically as possible.

Like everyone else, she had heard of people going downhill fast, being ventilated and never waking up. She felt a rare moment of fear as she lay down on the cleared and cleaned stretcher a minute or two after the latest Covid-19 casualty had been removed. Was this it? Would she get up again under her own power? It seemed impossible to consider otherwise, but this morning she only felt like she had one of the constant colds that hung around this cursed place. As she shut her eyes she ehard the paramedic ask Sgt Andy Cunningham , who had just turned up, for her name. "It's alright Valerie, we'll look after you now, you just relax for the moment and breath.' She managed a grim-

ace at the familiarity in the paramedics use of her first name. As the lights went out in her mind, she heard Andy as if down a long tunnel, "shes a hard one this one, you'd better just stick with 'CS' ".

◆ ◆ ◆

Starfort 4 was built quickly and badly in early October 2020. It did not have to wait long to be tested. While other forts along the main Dublin Belfast road, for example, fairly effectively cut movement of insurgents and arms quite quickly, the more barren areas further into the rural heartland of the border region proved a physically harder but more reliable terrain over which to illicitly move people and things. From 'hiking groups' being tackled by 28 Battalion (Bn) troops in the mountains near Finner to the vehicle borne movements on the backroads further East, the Starforts very quickly grew in number and pace of activty. Patrolling from Starfort 4 was almost always on foot, although there was a small Quick Reaction Force (QRF) that had access to the Mowags that were allegedly there to use their optics as ISR equipment, but which everyone knew were really there for their Bushmaster cannons.

The immediate area was hills, woodlands, marshy swamps and general misery when it was cold and wet, as the Winter of 2020 notoriously was. While daytime activity was not out of the question, most of the illegal positioning of arms occured at night, being moved by road or by groups on foot. Initially, most of Starfort 4s patrols centred on putting up random roadblocks on the local roads crossing the border and this netted some succesful hauls, including a van full of mortar rounds. After the death on one of these checkpoints of Corporal (Cpl) Marty Andrews to sniper fire, the first death due to combat of an Irish soldier in the war, the patrol were either carried out less overtly or at much larger strength with either machine gun or sniper support or both for any checkpoint that might be required to linger in position. This was late October and the provision of mortar detachments, organic to the Starforts, had not yet been made.

This changed after the IRA decided that they needed to curtail or remove Defence Forces capabilities in the area, a total step change in comparison to the Troubles, where they sought to move under the radar as much as possible. This seems to have been borne both from increasing confidence in their new recruits and new weaponry and from the pressure they were under further North, whereby they had to have a secure route deeper into the Republic than the other groups could reach. Either way, a concerted effort was made through mortar fire, IEDs and heavy machine guns to render Starfort 4 ineffective, with this effort commencing in the second week of November 2020.

The Defence Forces pushed back of course and introduced both mortar and javelin missile support to the belegured fort. In addition, GPS jammers were quickly bought and pushed into service to deter drone attacks, much to the annoyance of the Air Corps who used GPS extensively in their helicopters, which constantly flitted about the border moving troops and supplies between forts and into the field.

It was worth pointing out that crews for both javelins and mortars were in short supply and high demand as pressure ramped up, both operationally and from the schools which required experienced trainers to push out reinforcements. A combination of indirect and direct fire reduced the effectiveness of direct attacks on the forts but did not stop them entirely. One favoured tactic of the local IRA, who had been given the task of opening this area for the overall use of their organisation, was to attack, withdraw and try to draw out the QRF into an ambush. To counter this, a system of 'leaving out' patrols at all times developed. If the attack happened close in, a 'left out' patrol would react before the QRF sometimes, grimly acting as a trip wire in case there were trip wires. Sgt Andy Cunningham relates one an account of one such patrol which went unexpectedly 'hot'.

Sgt Andy Cunningham

' So we were on a left out patrol, if you look North from Starfort 4, we were on the hills to the West, being about a kilometre and a half away maybe at the most from the Fort itself, and these hills formed nearly a continuous ridge around it, though it did have some low lying ground in between the hills, but generally the high ground went all the way around the fort on the Northern side.

It was a night patrol where it was raining, of course, being Cavan. We were, I suppose, 7 seven or maybe eight weeks into our allegedly three month stint up there now at this stage. People were getting into the swing of things, obviously we'd had some serious setbacks with the fatalities that had occurred by that stage and, yeah, it hadn't been a happy trip per se but I think people were still motivated about what we were doing there, you know. That was important too. Anyway tangents aside, we were on the top of the hills to the West ,kind of bedded down in some gorse which covered the entire top of that Hill, it was uncomfortable but kind of kept some of the rain off ,was a bit of concealment if not cover and we were just generally doing the usual, just waiting to see what happened to the front or in case anything else happened during the night back down towards the Fort itself.

Anyway it was after midnight. It was dark, so dark because there was no moon, very overcast and misty and rainy, as I say, when from the forward facing hill, that is to say that the side of the northern hill that was in view from Starfort 4 , there was what appeared to be a mortar and machine gun attack from the clearing in the centre of that wooded area.

Now obviously from day one, that area had been well laid in

as an area from which enemies could approach the fort quite closely. It was no more than about 300 meters away at its closest point, maybe about 500 from the from the clearing in the center of that wood . So obviously mortar, machine guns, everything was all laid in that area already, not really with the expectation that someone would attack from there. Prior to this, all the attacks had been from, you know kind of, I suppose sensible areas, tactically sound areas further out on the reverse slope of the hills where they couldn't be engaged directly with machine gunfire or even spotted immediately for mortars. For whatever reason, and I suppose it just indicates that even at this stage they were learning too maybe, for whatever reasons they hadn't properly taken on board some of the lessons that they had been instructed on and they attacked from this front slope of the hill.

From our position we obviously heard the thump of the mortars going off and the machine guns too but, like, no flash from the tubes or anything like that , it was just we weren't looking directly at it, you know, we were looking outwards onto the reverse side of the slope trying to cover off any approaches more so than anything else. So when we look over our shoulder, when we look back towards it, all we saw was the whole area lit up from the Starfort itself, we could you could hear the 'Tom Tom Tom Tom Tom' of the two Mowags engaging with the cannons and they seem to be engaging pretty much centrally in the clearing area, so the big flash of our mortars lighting up the area as well , you know you're trying to close one eye while you're looking at this to preserve your night vision.

As well as that, you could hear the clatter of the MAG SFs, that's a machine gun in the sustained fire role as it's called. These were mounted on tripods at the end of each point in the star of the fort and they were just working the whole area and you had what was clearly lads further back in the arms of the star engaging with GPMGs, that's General Purpose Machine Guns as well, the normal infantry GPMGs that you carry around and they seem to be just sweeping the outside area to try and catch anyone that tried to escape. So, in terms of the firepower going in there, you had 25mm Bushmaster cannons, 80mm mortars all centered on the area where the attack itself came from, and then you had 7.62mm sustained fire and infantry fire all just sweeping that whole wood. It would have been would have been a pretty horrible place to be I think, but I don't think any of us were feeling sorry for them at that stage.

Anyway, this went on for a good two minutes, which is a lot of ammunition. Especially when you talk about the heavy stuff. It died off bit by bit, first one then the other cannon and you could see the order going around by the tracer fire stopping, you know obviously lads we're having to get shouted at to stop shooting. I think everyone was, ah, everyone was keen to have a bit of a go back after what we'd been through over the last couple of weeks.

I'll be honest we were kinda cheering a little bit ourselves, the four of us in the patrol, until inevitably; because it was from the front slope it just looked like a come on, as if they had remotely fired because you wouldn't expect someone to go into that area and shoot. It looked like this had been remotely fired as a come on to get QRF out and engage them with something heavier, which was going to be scary if they were going to engage him with something heavier than what had already come out of the clearing.

So instead, we were told to patrol into the area confirm whether it was a remote attack or not, and then pull out leaving it for the QRF. Remote attacks, that happened. One of their favorites was to stick an old weapon, pre ceasefire era weapons into a tube then cut off the trigger guard and it have a little battery and an irregularly shaped cam that would be activated by mobile phone, and this cam would turn around and would actually hit the trigger, release it, hit the trigger, release it so that it seemed like you were getting the kind of bursts of twos and threes, making it look like there was a human behind it but when you got close it was just a pipe. Very hard to find and of course generally there was some form of IED underneath when you did get close, just in case you were stupid enough to pick it up.

So, back to the story. We did proceed tactically, but we did fairly hustle as well, to get over there. Once we got to the wooded area or just before it, we stopped got it together and then proceeded with a bit more care. It was evident, even at night it was evident, under NVGs that we were using just how much damage had been done to the area and you could still hear hot metal sizzling in the rain. There were fresh strike marks on the trees, some branches cut off entirely just by GPMG fire and that was just on the outside of the wooded area itself. The further you progressed the more hellish it became. Approaching the area around the clearing, and where we might have expected to start encountering survivors or IEDS or anything, there was nothing, but it was pretty clear that anything in that area had been taken out. At that point I was concerned about secondary explosions, if anything was still burning, any ammunition that might still go off and injure the team.

Once we got into the area of the mortar pit itself, you could look around from there and you could see the fort quite clearly, and you know it was it was quite frightening that, to see how under observation we were on a day-to-day basis, but anyway in this pit itself that's where we found remains of the mortar crew. Very badly shot up, very disassembled would be the word I'd use, by the incoming fire. It was impossible to tell what had done it, was it the mortars or whatever, but I think a lot of it was done by the direct fire cannons on the Mowags, just from the way the ground was chewed up. It was four people that we saw altogether in just in that one area, all dead. All dead straight away, don't believe what you're reading online that we were executing people after the fact, there was none of that nor need for it.

We carried on, obviously, to search the wooded area. We called it in first of course, but carried on just a search of the area around the clearing and we found more guys in there who, when the rounds started coming in, there was two guys that made a run for it. They, they were all shot up by 7.62 and that was my first time seeing people, in four overseas trip that was my first time seeing people that had been shot up quite so badly. Obviously, our own guys during the course of the previous weeks, but that was a different thing. It had quite an effect I have to say, not just on me on some of the younger boys that were there as well. But they held it together, they did the job right, the area was cleared and we called it in and then we drew back out to the edge of the woods until the QRF came in and sealed off the area and at that point we were brought back into the fort itself.'

The action described above by Sgt Andy Cunningham is typical of the events of the time. The IRA were attempting to assert themselves in the area, but despite the influx of equipment and existing command elements, they were still making some mistakes due to the inexperience of their newer members. The Defence Forces capitalised on this at each opportunity. It also shows how the full complement of Air Corps ISR assets had not yet been deployed to provide 24/7 coverage and indeed that the ground based ISR assets were also spread thinly. This sometimes meant that the enemy could get quite close.

He also describes that the sight of dead people on the enemy side had an effect on him. With the same soldiers often rotating through the same areas more frequently than intended and with few opportunities to rest, this was a problem that grew too – soldiers were seeing not only enemy dead, they were watching their own comrades die as well. The death count for the Black Winter exceeded that which Ireland sustained throughout the whole of the Troubles, but on top of that there were the many injured. These deaths and injuries not only had a direct emotional effect on troops, it had the secondary effect of creating more vacancies which had to be filled, meaning the same soldiers were back on the border again very quickly.

Every combat arm unit in the army had provided troops to the counter insurgency fight in one way or another and had sustained that effort. The ability to rotate troops was low and the demand was high. In addition to witnessing death, soldiers were now being called on to fire back in numbers which the DF had not been used to in quite some time. This too had an effect over time. Sgt Dan Morris recounted the first time he had to open fire at someone in an interview shortly before his death:

Sgt Dan Morris

'I do remember the first time alright; I don't think you forget, or not easily anyway. I was on a patrol, standard daytime left out patrol near Starfort 11. We were moving along the edge of a wood, there was a clear area of fields about 50m wide between us and another wooded area running parallel, maybe a bit less than that. We were back in a bit into the trees, just to be out of sight, when we picked up movement the other side, they were more or less straight across from us! My first thought was, 'they're patrolling like us, like they own the place' and I was a bit affronted I suppose by that, but from their perspective I guess it would've made sense.

There was four of them, two with big backpacks of kit which turned out to be explosives, two more with AKs. I was about to call it in as a QRF job, weight of numbers and all that, when one of the young lads decides he's going to challenge them like he's on the gate into barracks or something. They saw him, probably not the other three of us in the treeline and everyone froze for a second, to see what would happen next 'cos the fella that shouted worked out he'd made a mistake as soon as he opened his mouth. One of them went to raise his rifle and we all hit the ground and fired. I saw the guy with the raised rifle go down straight away, but that wasn't me. I was shooting at the other guy with a rifle who had worked it out and gotten down as well. I hit him too. The guys with the backpacks could probably have just legged it into the woods and gotten away, instead one of them picked up the rifles and threw them into the open, they surrendered! We were surprised by that, but I guess a bag full of bomb on your back is good motivation to not get shot at.

Anyway, we ceased fire and, it's a strange thing; whenever you stop firing a Steyr rifle, there's this vibration in the springs in the butt of the gun that you feel through your cheekbone as much as hear it. And that was the same then as it was on the rifle range or on exercises or anything else. It was just so strange to feel something so familiar in such a new circumstance and that brought me back to reality. I called for an ammo/cas – how much ammo do you have left and are you wounded – from my own lads and then we secured the prisoners. We called in a med-evac heli for their wounded, the two boys with rifles were still alive, one chest wound and I had hit the other fella in the head. He was barely conscious, the round had hit the rifle before him. It was a very uncomfortable thing to experience, here's this guy lying in blood and I did it to him. Regardless of the context.'

The continual degradation of Starfort 4, through casualties, disease and sheer unsuitability to it's task ultimately led to a number of dramatic and well needed changes in the organisation of the physical defence of the border and the Defence Organisation itself. I say this despite the fact that many in the Defence Forces will not use the term and seek to distance themselves from the Department of Defence (DoD). By the middle of December 2020, the unit occupying the fort had to be relieved. In the harsh winter, they had simply run out of available bodies. Although further casualties would be suffered over the coming months, the bulk of the damage had already been done. All four of the fatal injuries and eighteen of the twenty four casualties through direct combat action and all of the Covid-19 related casualties had been inflicted on C Coy of 2 Bn North Central (The border Bns were comprised of troops from various units in the Defence Forces in the same manner as overseas units, but stepped outside the established numbering system. To further confuse issues, AO's or Areas of Operation sometimes overlapped with existing units, for example 2 Bn North Central overlapped in Leitrim with the existing 28 Bn based in Finner and there was no '3 Bn West').

The dissolving of C Coy, which was already understrength to start was used as an excuse not to press charges when, as is now almost beyond doubt and widely accepted, the remaining buildings in Starfort 4 were put to the torch when the unit withdrew. If there was no C Coy, there could be no OC C Coy to charge. This logic was contested loudly at a meeting between the Minister for the Defence and Foreign Affairs, the Chief of Staff and a member of the DOD who was attending on behalf of the the, still new, Secretary General of the Department. When the DOD member suggested that the fort would be rebuilt from existing funds and more soldiers found to occupy it, the breifing officer allegedly replied that the fort would only be occupied by soldiers walking over a carpet of civil servants, in light of their lack of concern for the wellbeing of members of the Defence Forces, or so the story goes.

Apocryphal or not, it was following that meeting that the decision was made, on the Ministers recommendation, that Defence be seperated from Foreign Affairs and a fulltime minister employed. That this minister was almost immediately produced as a Taoiseach's nomination to the Seanad suggests that this was not the first time this had been discussed. The fact that an ex Army Brig Gen could be appointed as a Senator out of sequence with the normal timeline, and with very little political opposition, suggests that cross party support had already been felt out for such a move.

Before touching on the practical effects of the death of Starfort 4 – which was loudly claimed by the IRA as a victory - it is worth discussing the major impact that the appointment of Sen Davis to the role of Minister for Defence had. Formerly Brig Gen Davis (a rank he held based on appointments held overseas as a force commander with the UN, his highest domestic appoinment having been Director of Strategic Planning Branch in DFHQ) had a long career in the Defence Forces including the usual assortment of overseas trips and commands before retiring in 2016. His subsequent career as an advisor to the boards of several companies who had personnel and interests in conflict areas meant that he had maintained a discrete but still observable profile.

As the likely scale of the post Brexit violence began to become apparent, tentative agreements were made to entice him into service again. Specifically, he was given a very free hand to reform things in both the civil and military side of the defence house, on the grounds that his fulltime retirement would follow his appointment. As if to lay down the ground rules for the change in culture that was going to be required, the Senator, as his very first act and with his seal of office from the president still in hand, called the Sec Gen of the DOD and instructed that arrangements be made with immediate effect for the issuing of medals to the soldiers who fought at Jadotville, exactly in line with their commanding officer Comdt Pat Quinlans recommendations. This was well received in the Defence Forces but with some unease in the Department he now ran. Nevertheless the point was made that past wrongs can be put to right quickly if you really want to, and that changes can happen fast with the right drive and application of streamlined decsion making.

The cleaning out and retirement of senior members of the DOD has been attributed various actors including the Senator, the new Sec Gen and even the Red Team, but there is little doubt that within a very short period of time, policy in the Defence Organisation was directed by the minister and that the Chief of Staff and his advisors were far more empowered than previously had been the case. The Senator also surrounded himself with advisors who were experts in their fields. One of the most prominent was another former member of the Defence Forces who had served as an enlisted man in the Army before moving into the field of research and development. His specialist focus was on one thing – process acceleration.

Putting the assembled skills around him to work, the Senator directed an accelerated build up of forces, including first and second line reserves, the second line being the 'new FCA' and the first line being both ex regulars and 'special skills servicemen/women'. The new FCA would eventually be formed with an establishment of 20,000 (this has never been reached no matter how many times it has been quoted, the highpoint was 6,000). The first line reserve 'SSS' soldiers, which as has been often said is one small typo short of catastrophe, largely consisted of various I.T. trained personnel who became the 29th Cyberwarfare Bn. The ex regulars in the first line reserve included the Red Team, although they adopted an old FCA Battalion number. Transparency and consistency with existing norms never became their strongpoint.. The policy and strategy of securing the border was laid out early on, it was up to the existing personnel however to buy the time for the build up to take effect. With the policy and strategy being deliberatly kept out of circulation, it required discipline and motivation on the part of the Defence Forces rank and file when morale was already being battered.

CHAP 3

Friction 1

The crash and recovery of Echo 292

Jan 2021

It was raining. Just misty, sticking to the hills crap, but apparently that had been enough. Cpl Diane Keane had never seen combat up to now, she'd done one tour in the Leb more or less straight out of recruit training and before all this kicked off. It had been a quiet trip according to the old sweats, but enough to give her an extra bump on her NCOs course. That came early enough in the twenty two year olds' career but there were plenty of NCO vacancies to be filled. Either way she wasn't sure if this even counted as combat per se.

She wiped off the salty sweat that the rain was washing down her forehead and into her eyes and shook her helmet with one hand to try and scratch an itch right on the hotspot where it sat on the top of her scalp. There was still fuck all to see though, but they'd heard it. The EC135 helicopter had meant to be part of their ISR cover for a Coy strength (well big platoon, but who's counting) patrol of eastern part of the Cooley Mountains. It had been delayed due to the weather but after a bit of pressing by Bn HQ the pilot decided to 'have a look'. They were up near the ridgeline east of Long Womans Grave and should have been able to see across into Warrenpoint and Rostrevor in the North, and Greenore at the bottom of the hill they were standing on, but all they could see was about twenty metres in front of them.

Whatever had happened to the helicopter, she knew immediately something had gone wrong. She could hear the usual slap of blades they made when they turned, before the sound increased in pitch and volume before lowering again and then returning with a vengeance. The actual explosion itself was different than she would have thought, the shout that went up in the patrol meant she wasn't the only one who knew it was coming, or the only one with the sudden fear of where it might land because it seemed like it was all happening right above them. The noise when it came; they were all familiar with the snap of rifles, the crack of a supersonic round passing over your head and even the boom of rapidly expanding gases from high explosive going off, but this, this was more of a 'whomp' noise. You'd imagine it should have been quieter than the others, but it wasn't and it still felt like being kicked in the back. She could feel the shockwave go through her when the fuel went up on impact.

It seemed like an age but couldn't have been even a minute before they came on the scene. Or bits of it anyway. She passed pieces of smouldering matt green composite material from the tailboom on the ground. Bits of the peat bog surface of the hill were torn up and gouged by what had obviously been fast moving metal and ahead a orange glow in the mist told them they were close.

Of the main part of the wreckage, there was one section that looked vaguely like the front of a helicopter in a fold in the earth, still burning and she couldn't see any other major components. She looked into the front section where the pilot should be, as close as she could get anyway, staying up wind of the fire – she could already see bits of burning fibres hanging in the air and didn't fancy breathing them in – one glance was enough, her brain gave an involuntary 'nope' warning that she knew meant it would wrap that memory in a ball and bury it deep and she turned back to her team. Lt Quinlan was already calling everyone back, telling them what they already knew now, that the pilot was dead, but also that they didn't know what weapons were on board or if there was any ammo to cook off in the fire. There wasn't as it turned out, apart from the pilots pistol, which was found still on him, but you don't take chances with that kind of thing. They fanned out and secured the area as much as they could, the wreckage was spread across a few hundred metres, vertically down the hill on the northern side as well as horizontally, and they had to try to stay in sight of each other. There wasn't a sniff of the enemy all day that day.

A number of realisations took place early in the Black Winter. One was that airborne ISR was going to be critical to fill in the gaps that could not only not be plugged by the available number of troops but also to maintain a bit of a degree of surprise, the ability to turn up anywhere at any time. The available drone technology worked reasonably well at a small unit tactical level, but better and bigger results were being achieved by the manned assets of the Air Corps. While the perceived gold standard for a patrol out along the border was one of the PC 12 Spectre fixed wing aircraft, these became increasingly unavailable due to being tasked for higher priority surveillance missions – this would change as more airframes were purchased. The fixed wing assets also lacked the flexibility of helicopters to get in beneath the frequent poor weather and still achieve the task.

The helicopters also provided a great degree of flexibiliy to Bn commanders to do everything from moving smaller patrols by air to resupplying Starforts to medevac and more. It didn't hurt that the helis of No 3 Ops Wing and the Army had worked together for years and mostly spoke the same language, or at very least were seperated by a common tongue to a lesser degree than with the fixed wing crews. The result was that No 3 Ops Wing was tasked with providing two helicopters on the border, one based in Dundalk and the other in Finner. This stretched an already under pressure unit to man these rosters and maintain training.

By the start of 2020, cadets were being sent overseas to conduct part of their heli training in order to accelerate the rate at which numbers of pilots were being produced. To provide aircraft for these new tasks, the existing two EC 135s in Air Corps service were supplemented by four leased airframes, while discussion commenced on how best to deal with the deployment long term. This did not however convey crucial flight experience on the pilots who, no matter how well trained, were being thrown raw into a demanding operational environment. Comdt Brian Rafferty , visibly upset during this portion of his interview, explains:

' An accident like that, look, the lads name was Dennis Ratigan – lets get that in for starts and stop just calling him 'the pilot' – an accident like that we call CFIT. That's controlled flight into terrain. Basically, what that means is that there was nothing wrong with the aircraft and that for whatever reason someone crashes. What happened in this case is called Inadvertent IMC. This means that the pilot, or Denny in this case, - I didn't know the chap well by any means I only met him a couple of times, that was just the nature of how things were going by that stage - he entered cloud without planning to and the result of that was that he lost control of the aircraft and crashed. This is actually a pretty common way for helicopter pilots in bad weather to go out. And regardless of your experience level, it's an extremely difficult scenario to get yourself out of safely, especially if you made the wrong moves early in the sequence.

What happened? Eh, what happened appears to be that he made the right decision early on, at the start of the morning and that was when he said he couldn't go because the weather was too bad in the area. He could, you could see it straight after you took off from Dundalk. But as sometimes happens you know, operational pressures come in. In this case from the Battalion HQ and, well, it's a brave 2 Lt who decides he's not going to fly then, even though that's what we drill into them repeatedly at home. He trained overseas so I'm not as sure how much emphasis is on it elsewhere? In this case, he departed on his own, because we had a shortage of crewmen at the time too, presumably with the intention that he would go up, have a look at the area: if it could be worked he'd work it, if not, just turn around. It was clear air in Dundalk, he had no reason to think he won't be able to do so.

As he approached the southern side of the Cooley Mountains the weather was down, we know from the flight data recorder that he was already below the level of the patrol that he was meant to be overhead and supporting, you know? He slowed down, got low in close to the mountain, nearly in a hover and tried to work his way up towards the patrol. For whatever reason, whether he was distracted by something or I dunno what else, he entered cloud at that stage.

Had he broken away to the South immediately, you know, he would have come out of the cloud and he would have been fine but he simply pulled in all the power, and at low airspeed in a helicopter all that's going to happen there, without countering that power, is you're going to spin in circles and that's what happened. He was pretty much in the hover, that's what happened, and he went straight up in the air spinning.

To listen to the flight data recorder, as I had to do as part of the accident investigation, is pretty horrifying. He climbed straight up as I said, the aircraft was spinning, and from his perspective you know the dials and the airspeed and altitude tapes, you know, they would have been just going all over the place because by now he was rolling and pitching all over the place as well. Really swift rates of movement which would just totally throw your ears off balance, not an unusual thing in cloud in itself if you move too aggressively without looking at your instruments, but we were talking 90 degrees nose down, 60 degrees angle a bank and ,you know, even going over past 90 degrees at some stages, um.

It appears, you know, you can hear him shouting on the flight data recorder, as well trying to understand what's going on in front of him and it's clearly, clearly overwhelmed him. Maybe; I hope that he was just confused all the way to the ground, that he didn't realize what was happening. Um, the end result was that he impacted the mountain. The crumple zones of the helicopter pretty much couldn't do their job because he came down sideways, the aircraft wrapped itself up, it impacted on a slope and the aircraft exploded and came apart. The cockpit section didn't actually move too far, but the engine's spread out along the hill, the main gearbox we found actually 200 meters down the hill, significantly far away, and the recording stopped, obviously, on impact That was a grim day in the unit, no getting around saying something like that. This was a young guy who hadn't had a chance yet to really make an impact, you know a lot of us, like I said, we didn't actually know him much, hadn't met him socially really, just kind of passed him in the halls. We'd be on our way to our job and he was going to Dundalk or Finner. But, it had a massive impact obviously on his classmates in particular.

The recovery of the aircraft was hampered in the initial part by the weather, but also because of where it was, we were under observation from the northern side; and we knew we were being watched just because of where the wreckage was. So the security situation dictated a fairly brief accident investigation at that scene. There was a lot of security put down in order to let the civilian Air Accident Investigation Unit (AAIU), the civilian air accident investigation unit in to see it. That was considered important to have them there, to still maintain that transparency at a time when things were changing quite rapidly for the military and for the civilian population.

Once the wreckage was released to us, one of our Heli Handling Teams went in and prepared the load itself into what are called single use bags, these are essentially like builders' bags and they were prepared into that for us to remove it. It's not as simple as it sounds. Due to the way modern aircraft are made and what they're made from, it's a hazardous enough environment for those teams to be working in, and obviously they helped with the removal of 2nd Lt Ratigan as well. He was taken off the mountain by a medevac aircraft with as much of a guard of honour as could be given under the circumstances. But the aircraft itself, that that was removed in what is essentially a small shipping container. An AW139 would cargo sling this container into position, the 'builders bags' would then be manhandled into this container and sealed.

Aircraft recoveries are notoriously difficult to carry out from mountains, especially as the wind had picked up that day towards 20 knots, there was a history in the unit of those loads being dropped, and that's where the box came in. It just flew like a box all the time, regardless of the wind or what was in it. So, yeah, the loads were just stuck in the box and away we went with it down to a field on the southern side, where it was unloaded and driven away by trucks. The main gearbox was a different challenge, that was 200 meters down the hill on the northern side, it had been substantially damaged in the impact and we ended up rolling that into single use bags and winching it out in the end ,which was a more novel way of doing things . In a small tight unit like No 3 - we didn't lose as many over the Black Winter as some of the infantry units - but those kinds of things had a major, major effect on people and the unit going forward.'

Interlude: The Red Team: Origin and recruitment

It was raining. Capt David Healy was having a bad weekend. Forming up for an overseas trip was always busy and tough but this was by far the worst he'd seen in his twelve years and three trips. MREs were meant to train, test and assess each travelling Bn on the skills they would need in their respective AOs. By necessity, to get through all the different skill sets required, they could be fairly scripted affairs. This one was turning out differently. As an experiment, an extra free play exercise of 72hrs duration was added to the middle of the programme against an unspecified unit, which had free reign to operate as they wished with the resources they were given – roughly the same as what might be encountered overseas.

His Bn commander and most of the staff element had 'died' after 4 hrs. A feint attack on an outlying village had drawn out the QRF and their armour. Although frequently patrolled, the area around the main FOB on Cemetery Hill in the Glen of Imaal had been found clear and the remaining troops in the HQ were rotating in and out as they eased into the standard pattern of life that goes with any base. Sleep, patrol, plan, sleep, patrol.

This was observable, however, and at about noon, the suppressed noise of a helicopter could be heard behind a 'cleared hill'. Shortly thereafter there was a series of thumps as the HQ came under fire from the mortar team that had just been dropped into position. As staff troops ran to their fighting positions, which were spaced out quite a bit by the absence of the QRF, the DS or Directing Staff said the three things every soldier in exercise hates to hear 'Gas, Gas, Gas!'.

The simulated mortars now carried a mix of deadly chemical weapons which the DS were simulating with actual tear gas (this was new to most people on the exercise, you normally only saw real CS during training in the aptly named gas chamber in the Curragh). Anyone with red eyes was quickly being declared dead, including by this point the Bn Commander, who was a bit tardy with getting his mask on. To round things off, the noise of helis returned but closer this time. As two landed, one circled the camp, strafing with door guns anyone who had lingered in the open to fit their gas masks. It swapped with one of the recently landed helicopters and in this way, working in concert, a platoon strength force of enemy troops with one 80mm mortar had beheaded their Battalion in less than twenty minutes before fading away under cover of machine gun fire from above..

That was Friday. It had of course gotten worse, as the other companies were kept occupied in their areas by sporadic sniper fire and IEDS. This was Sunday evening and through a series of attacks, feints and misdirections, 'his' QRF company (the actual CO having been sniped along with the CQ on Saturday night) was now down to two dismounted platoons, no armour and no recce teams. The third platoon had gone to the rescue of the last of the recce element the previous afternoon only to join them in being decimated by ambushing enemy troops.

He led his Orders group through his plan to break out on foot back to Cemetery Hill where they would hold until reinforced. The sun fell low over the Glen and as the darkness enveloped the near slopes in shadow, coordinated sniper fire rang out just as he asked 'Any questions?'. As one, the TESS gear, a sensor system designed to detect a laser simulating a bullet, being worn by the O group squealed that they'd been hit and wouldn't stop until they lay down flat on the dirt. As further volleys of fire echoed around the hills, the sound of helicopters once again joined the high pitched noise of more of his 'dead' soldiers.

Distinctly pissed off, Heally cursed into the dusk. The Red Team were winning. That wasn't meant to happen.

Comdt Dave Heally

'The origins of the Red Team as they came to be known were already getting fuzzy by the time I was recruited. The accepted version is that they were initially a bunch of exers brought in to lecture on the Command and Staff course in around 2014 or so, this being to make up for the experience that was already leaving the DF at the time. From guest lecturing, they moved on to acting as the enemy staff when the class would be doing their exercises – up to that apparently, some students were seen to take a fairly easygoing approach to them. They'd draw an arrow on the map and that was your axis of advance for your armour, never mind the state of the roads kind of thing.

All of a sudden there was a bunch of people in a different room responding and working against them and there were a few embarassing results. For those first few exers, it was all a bit of craic; they'd no worries about promotions or anything and it was all a bit of nostalgia and catching up with the lads. It was also a bit cool on your Linkedin page : OPFOR at Command and Staff School , Military College. They were the first 'Red Team' as they called themselves.

After a while, one of them during a debrief or a chat with the COS or something put up the idea of doing real world tests on the DF, the reasoning being that they were saying that most of the exercises they'd been on in their own time in uniform were overly scripted and lacked the chaos of freeplay that would challenge leaders in the field. They were given a company of reservists and a few supporting assets that they asked for and told to go squeeze it in to an upcoming MRE. That was 2016 and lo and behold, a super secret death squad was born. Allegedly. Rumour had it they were recruiting personnel onto their staff over the course of those MRE's as well. Someone would get a text or an email towards the end of their subsequent trip saying, hey you should come hang out with us, you'll stay in one place for a few years and won't get moved from pillar to post as much. That would be enough to keep a lot of guys you know, a bit of stability at home. Anyway, I never got a call – probably 'cos they killed me!

I say that because, at some point and this is where it all gets a bit murky, a few of the more serious individuals were hived off and began doing risk assesments. By risk assesments, I mean they were told to go and plan terrorist attacks on national infrastructure, or just given a specific effect to achieve and off you go. Needless to say, when ministers or sec gens in certain departments were handed reports saying 'you've fucked up and are massively exposed here and here and look at these pictures' they'd immediately counter that these were only paper exercises and wouldn't actually work because, you know , magic or something.

At that point, the Red Team guys were allowed bring in a small number of people to act on their behalf with the only provision being that they must use military or ex military and they couldn't actually put bombs near civilians. They still made the bombs to prove the point that they could get what they needed to do it, but they blew them up in the Glen. When people think of the Red Team now, this is probably the core group that spawned it. By the end of 2017, they had apparently crippled the country with cyber attacks, taken out HVTs more or less at will and created terror amongst the population, all pretend of course.

When things went hot, they were looked on as a bit of a think tank with the potential to be more muscular. No one really knows from there, but what I've heard is that the Transport Bombings in Dublin were more or less a carbon copy of one of their plans. That was a bit of a fuck you from the Russians, which means that their planning was compromised and the Russians had something to be pissed about. Probably someone disappeared one too many Russian facilitators in the North. I mean, that's what people say happened anyway, who knows.'

Friction 2

Starfort 11 , March 2021

Pte Thomas McLanahan was on guard in Starfort 11. The weather wasn't as bad as it had been all winter but that didn't mean much. It was foggy, as usual, maybe more of a wet mist. The cold, slowly soaking you anyway kind, that left you freezing in your core and made it hurt to move if you stayed still for any length of time. Guard duty here was especially shit. On a left out patrol, even if nothing was happening, if you were still freezing, you were at least mentally occupied in your role as a human tripwire. QRF duty, there were a few of you knocking around idly shit talking, to cover for the sense of just under the surface tension of having to go out if something did go off. Guard duty though, too much time in your own head.

Each fort had a 'guardroom' an actual block building in some, in this case a portacabin with its back to the wall, near the forts' entrance and with earth and sandbags piled all the rest of the way around it. He was standing on 'the beat'; a walkway (mud actually) with sandbags piled in a wall up to about chest height and a corrugated tin roof where you would move around to actually see what was going on. Everyone took their own few hours on the beat and while they did, the rest of the guard would either be on camera watch looking at the cctv, their phones or realistically, asleep.

It had not been an easy few years for Tom McLanahan. After the reorg of 2012, his home barracks, that he had trained in and grew up near, had been shut down and he'd been moved to Athlone. This meant commuting, which ate up too much of his reduced paycheck that had never quite recovered to pre austerity levels, no matter how much politicians promised to 'look at it' during the next review . This in turn meant sleeping in the barracks and when the accomodation block was being renovated, sleeping in his car. Things weren't easy at home, abscence in this case not making the heart grow fonder , or maybe it was just all the extra stress of it all, living paycheck to paycheck but things had ended badly with his then fiance. She wasn't his biggest fan since then either. If he was honest with himself, he probably did start drinking too much at the time, skipped out on one too many runs, put on too much weight and that led to him doing in his ankles when he eventually did get onto a potential NCOs course, which as his CO said to him directly, was a bone thrown to him as a chance to straighten himself out. He lost most of the weight but never tried for another course since, figured his luck wasn't in it.

As the lads around him moved on, got married, had kids, got promoted, he found himself increasingly alone. Still drinking a bit too much, though, and by now the oldest Pte living in in the barracks. The wasn't strictly through, actually, it's just that he was the oldest one that was always there – the other living in guys had hobbies, things to do that weren't behind the bar in the mess. After a while, each new set of younger soldiers in the place got bored of being his drinking buddies of the week and did their own thing too. By this stage, he knew, he just knew, the NCO's and the older guys were pointing him out as that guy who was a 'nice enough lad, but don't end up propping up the bar with him'. The guy to avoid if you can. He still got on well enough with them all during the day alright, but the nights were long and it didn't take much temptation to drown the voices in the back of his mind telling him it should all be better than this.

That, of course, was before everything had gone to shit in the country. Covid-19 19 had shut the place down and then the border kicked off again. It wasn't too bad at first, when they were working out of Dundalk and Finner, bit of extra cash and with everyone staying in,there was a few of the old sweats like him around. For about three weeks it was just like the old days. Then they were sent to that bastard of a place in Cavan, Starfort 4. And then the killing started. No amount of good intentions could make that place happy, but certainly a blood sacrifice hadn't done the trick either.

It was bad enough if someone went out and didn't come back, but the lads that died in camp... he'd held Sgt Pete Foster when he died. The usual harassing mortar fire came in and just that day Pete was slower getting into a dugout. Took a handsized fragment through the back which barely slowed for the back plate of his body armour before going through his abdomen and nearly bursting out through the front plate. Tom had run out from cover and grabbed his hand to drag him back in, but Pete had just held on to him and looked up at him. He knew himself he was done, he knew. Impending doom, the paramedics had called it after, that feeling of certainty that you were going to die. The look on his face stayed with Tom from that day on though. Fear. Pain. And stupid amounts of snot, just in case the point of stripping him of his dignity and life hadn't already been made. No words though, he was too badly messed up inside and was, in fact, drowning in his own blood, whatever of it wasn't running out into the mud.

The boss, Lt Quinlan told him afterwards that he was recommending him for a medal after that. He hadn't even noticed himself that the mortars were still coming. But he'd known Pete since they were seventeen, twenty years nearly. Alright, they hadn't hung out much recently (or longer, really) but even after things had gone off the rails for him, Pete had been around. He'd tried a couple of times to help him back on his feet. Who wants a medal for that? He was trying to help his friend. It should be a given.

It was at the funeral, he'd at least gotten away from the border for that, that things really hit him first. Pete's family were there. His wife Marianne who, truth be told, had probably laid out for Pete exactly what to say to help him was there, but she was barely recognisable. She'd always been so bubbly, but he could tell that was gone now. There was the usual ceremony, shots over the grave etc, but he hadn't been part of the official proceedings. He just stood towards the back of the crowd that spilled onto the street. And that was when it hit him. The crowd that turned out for Pete was huge because he was loved. Who'd be there for him if they'd swapped parts in that days drama? Who's life would be changed for ever if he was gone? He'd left the graveyard at that point and was already several pints in when the rest arrived at the pub. But the idea stuck in his head, like a parasite burowing deeper and deeper. If he was gone, who'd even know?

Coming back up Starfort 4 the next day was an exercise in even greater misery than usual. Like everyone else, he was happy when the place was burned. Maybe just satisfied at seeing it get what it deserved rather than happy. But Starfort 11 was just down the road, wasn't it. Combining the remains of the two originally understrength companies that had occupied both forts brought the total people there to one, still understrength, infantry company. And it seemed like it would never end. Patrols, mortars, IEDS, Covid-19 and lads not coming back in.

Sometime between 0315 and 0330 on the night of March 04 2021, Pte Thomas McLanahan cocked his rifle, put the muzzle in his mouth and fired.

Lt Brian Quinlan

'I remember that night, obviously. I was duty officer – in charge of the general security within the fort as opposed to QRF or anything – the same as being orderly officer in any barracks except smaller but more likely to go wrong. If anyone was going outside, I'd be the one signing out the weapons in the armoury and that kind of thing. I was also responsible for our own camp guard and arranging medevacs, so... two for the price of one that night. I remember afterwards in the investigation people, asking me was there anything off about him or anything noticeable and I nearly laughed at them – everything was off about everyone by that point, anyone who'd been in Starfort 4 especially. But no – to give the actual answer I gave them – there was nothing out of place when I last saw him alive.

I thought we were under attack initially when I heard the shot, but there was just one and, by that point we could kind of tell, you know? The vibe around the place was instantly wrong. My duty room was in a portacabin across the helipad in the centre of the camp, over near the armoury itself and the canteen. When I ran outside, I was the only one moving, no alarm, no shouts, no more shots. Just that quiet you get when you know someone is dead.

I got up to the beat and the guardroom and, well, it was quite a graphic scene. I had to push one of the younger Ptes out of the way – he was new and had never seen anything like it – I could see myself then that... I could see that his helmet had been blown off of his head and was lying upside down near the wall of sandbags. The back of his head was largely gone and he had pure black eight ball eyes. He was gone, I mean that was immediately obvious. I could see that someone had removed the rifle from his mouth, which you're not meant to do, you know, for the MP investigation and all that, it's technically a crime scene until proven to be suicide so they need it left alone. But, eh, one of his buddies there that knew him from Mullingar was on guard with him and had been the first one out and he started trying to give him CPR. Cpl Tyrrel was guard commander and he had him still restrained from trying to get at the body again. The strap on his helmet, I mean – it's funny what you see, what sticks with you afterwards, the strap on his helmet was still closed at the clasp but was broken at the end where it attaches to the helmet itself. That was the force of the shot at that range.

That, I think, was the last straw and whatever morale was left in the place was gone. I'm not going to lie, he was a guy who had his problems, but he was liked well enough by nearly everyone and a solid soldier, never seemed afraid anyway. It really affected the unit badly to be honest, that kind of shit justs radiates out through everyone around it.'

The Medical Corps of the Defence Forces saw rapid and sustained growth throughout the wars, especially the reserve elements which gave doctors the chance to see things they simply wouldn't in the general community, without having to give up their permanent jobs. But if trauma docs treating gunshot wounds as weekend warriors became something of a meme in the medical community, the same cannot be said for the mental health side of the house. This group found it much harder to recruit and resource its increasing needs. The Defence Forces own PSS – Personnel Support Services – soon found themselves swamped during the Black Winter. As the battle for finite funds and time increased, invisible services like PSS were not so much forgotten about as not increased to the same scale as the operational units.

While the PSS initially focussed on providing resilience training for troops going to the border as part of their predeployment training, the amount of 'critical incidents' that required a mandatory debrief soon outnumbered those trained to lead that debrief in any kind of reasonable time. As troops began to do back to back tours, or from their point of view, simply staying where they were, critical incidents for each unit began to 'store up', leading to them being dealt with all in one day as PSS staff visited each unit.

This meant that they sometimes encountered a certain level of bitterness from soldiers, who were being asked to recount and relive it all in one go and who felt that their own loss was being dealt with as a tickbox exercise, rather than being recognised at the level it might have been in peacetime. Where PSS staff recommended that DF associated social workers follow up in certain cases, the back log meant that the timeline involved ran to close to two years, even in this first phase of the war. The PSS staff for their own part, suffered themselves with exposure to so many horror stories without having the resources to help.

It has become now a recognised reality, that by bearing so much of the initial load of the wars on so few shoulders, the Defence Forces has activated a timebomb that is both detonated and ticking at the same time. It will continue to exist in this state for a long time to come as each soldier gradually comes to terms with what they have seen and done.

Interlude : QRA, the British withdraw, enter the French

The provision of a Quick reaction Alert force for policing Irish airspace, both over land and out over the Atlantic was one that in theory came to a head during the political arguments post Brexit, but in fact had been bubbling away just below public consciousness for some time. In the same way as peacekeeping is not a job for soldiers, but only soldiers can do it, an air policing capability can only be provided if you have fighter jets capable of sustained highspeed and with the range to make it matter. People saw fighter jets and straight away thought 'why do we need them , we're neutral?' The notion of intercepting an aircraft that was not identifying itself over the sea and escorting it so that every airliner in the area could know where it was and avoid it was a bit abstract for many.

Equally, the notion that proclaiming neutrality actually meant increasing your military obligations was a step too far for a country where defence spending was just not on peoples radar at all. Successive governments looked at the issue, looked at the cost and then looked away. In the aftermath of 9/11, a secretive deal was drawn up between the DoD, the IAA and the UK MOD to provide QRA over Ireland via the RAF. Notably absent from the conversation were the Irish Air Corps. The cost borne by the state, rules of engagement over Ireland or in Irish controlled airspace or the issue of whether or not it was constitutional for foreign forces to operate in Ireland without Dail permission were never explored in public. It is likely that they now never will be as the capability was unilateraly withdrawn by the UK during the Winter of 2020, the infamous Black Winter.

At the time, this was intended to put presure on Ireland to modify the EU position on some of the trade deal negotiations which had reached an impasse. It was not succesful ironically because of the low value put on conventional Defence issues by Irish politicians, even then when the war against the IRA was building in intensity on the border and there was an increasing amount of intercepts of Russian TU 95 and TU 142 Bear aircraft on the west coast. In hindsight, while some of these aircraft were providing support for Russian undersea operations around the fibre optic cables that arrived in Europe at the Porcupine Banks, others were undoubtedly recceing the country for the drop zones for the subsequent weapons deliveries that accelerated the war.

Perhaps seeing the danger more clearly than the Irish political leadership, the French government offered to take up the role. Whereas the UK had been able to provide the service from their own bases in Britain, the extra distance involved meant that the French sent a detachment of Rafale aircraft and two tankers to Shannon. Arriving in March 2021, the fighters alternated between different French air force and naval squadrons and used the airspace offshore to conduct some of their own training, along with some training in support of Defence Forces units. While it is clear that the purpose of the detachment was only ever intended to be air policing, the presence of French military jets based in Ireland was to have a significant impact on the course of later events and almost ended in war between the UK and the EU/ French.

The friendly and expensive gesture by France was not universally well received. Faced with no choice due to what was now an issue very much in the public eye, the Irish governement made the unusual decision to adopt without tender the quickest and cheapest option that could provide a capability in the increasingly demanding Irish air policing environment. This meant the wholesale adoption of the Swedish Air Force model via the Swedish Govt and Irish pilots of different ranks were sent to Sweden to learn to fly Gripen jets. Some were existing pilots who would fill out the staff and command role in the reactivated No 2 Fighter Wing. Others were brand new, straight from the PC 9M trainer used in the Air Corps own Flight Training School. Other still were Cadets taken early from their military training in the Curragh to be dropped into a soon to start Swedish AF basic flight training course. As with every other aspect of the Air Corps at the time, the system had a ravenous need for pilots and technicians that could not be met by existing training means.

The result was that it would be two years before the first Irish fighter jets went into combat, almost on delivery, in Ireland. In the meantime, the French were kept busier than they expected.

Friction 3

Early April 2021

The Sliabh Blooms

"You know this is someone else's killzone heed?" Pte Lukasz McGrath was standing straight up in the middle of the track, but at least keep-

ing a good watch out for his buddy, Pte Jan Nowak who was busy looking at the shell casings on the ground.

" I know , I'm just looking" . Jan had bent down and picked up one of the shell casings on the end of a pen and was examining it. On the bottom, he read off the calibre of the round- 5.45 X 39mm. " AK 74 maybe over here, not too many rounds fired"

" Plenty of 7.62 short over here in a pile beside the blood, I'd say this lad fired off everything and got clipped in the reload"

The two reservists were standing on a turn in the track with steeply wooded slopes rising behind their backs and also dropping away in front. The scene was mimiced across a narrow valley, more commercial forrestry, more trails, more blanket bog on the top of everything. As part of a PDF lead patrol, the two soldiers were recceing an area where a civilian hiker had reported shell casings and blood in an area where there had been no reported fighting during the clearing out operation of a fortnight ago.

"Alright CSI Laois/Offaly, tell me what you see." The instruction came over the earpiece of their personal radios from the patrol leader Cpl Diane Keane. Part of taking the new guys out on patrol in mixed units was teaching them things that had been cut out of the accelerated four month training. Part of that was basic recce skills and part of those was reading the ground and evidence in front of you to assess a situation and feed it back to their next level of command. Lukasz continued covering off while Jan, the bigger of the two spoke first.

" Well, whoever hit them up ambushed them on the turn to split the group. I'm seeing plenty of dried blood back around the turn – he gestured with a head movement, they'd already learned not to point – but not many rounds fired there, all 7.62 short so either one rifleman moving between two firing positions or two guys with rifles which would match up with the blood stains we can still see."

Lukasz took up the commentary-
" This side , we're seeing a bit more action. Like I said, I'd say one guy

fired a full mag and then got hit on the down slope side of the turn he was firing from. The 5.45mm stuff is in two piles, one near the up slope and one in the ditch on that side. Less rounds fired so probably taking aimed shots. At a pure guess, the blood in the middle of the track is his. I'd say he was nailed going to help his buddy after he got shot reloading."

" Good, anything else?"

Tucked back in the woods looking down on the site with the other four members of the patrol, Cpl Keane had already seen two important things they hadn't pointed out yet.
"Yeah" Jan took up the baton "There's drag marks here on the edge of the turn leading into the forest on the down sloping side, something heavy. Not a body, no blood and it's too regularly shaped. Mortar plate maybe?"

"Good, what else?"

"There's no one elses rounds here" Lukasz answered. " We haven't seen any 5.56 or 7.62 or even anyone elses rounds. So either they took all their own brass away or the firing points for the ambush were across the valley." He looked across at the trees on the other side more intently." Not bad from that distance, got to be 250, 300 metres and I'm not seeing the place here chewed up like you'd expect with machine gun fire"

"Good work, in terrain like this, you can't always tell the difference between machine gun fire and just heavy volumes of automatic rifle fire, but I concur it looks too tidy down here. Don't rule out coordinated sniper fire either. What does that tell you?"

"They didn't want to damage whatever they were after here with stray bullets "

" Correct, what else"

"We're still standing in someone elses killzone."

" They haven't shot you yet, but you're right. Back track along the trail a few hundred metres and then hop into the woods and rendezvous (RV) with us up here."

Pte McGrath and Pte Nowak were from Monaghan and were some of the first batch of the reserves of the 'new FCA' that had been released into the wild of operations after four months of training. They'd spent the last six weeks since they came out of training on patrols around rural Monaghan, basically the first part of the plan to relieve the PDF members there since the previous year. As unemployed former meat factory workers, they were two of the many 'full time' part time soldiers that made up the 2nd Line Reserve as they were officially called. Of some note is that both were of Polish backgrounds, with Jan Nowak having moved to Ireland as a five year old and Lukasz McGrath having a Polish mother. This is only of note as the reserves came to be composed of a disproportionate number of people who had either immigrated themselevs or who had parents who had come to Ireland and stayed. Indeed, the unit raised from the area around Gort became known as 'The Boys from Brazil' and this was not meant in a derogatory fashion. The reasons why this might have been have been delicately debated and no clear cut answer has emerged. Perhaps the answer is that they have as many reasons for joining the military as anyone else, for some it was a way of asserting that their Irishness is as valid as anyone elses, others had a history of military service in their families. Either way, in uniform, they proved they were Irish soldiers as much as anyone who could claim ancestory back to the Sons of Míl.

While most of the combat action took place close to the border, it was not restricted to that area. The event recounted above took place in the midlands two weeks after one of the most significant battles in modern Irish history. One which is sometimes overshadowed by the events in the Cooleys only a few weeks later. *Operation Garden Harvest* was a major effort to clean out and secure the Sliabh Blooms. While the focus of their activities remained on the border, the IRA knew they would forever be under the eye of both the Northern Irish and Irish security forces and the various illegal competitors who wanted to occupy that operational space. They needed a secure base to the south from where they could conduct operations – the old rules of the 'Green Book' had long since been cast aside and armed action against 'the Southern State' was now firmly on the menu. Normally, the sensible thing for an organisation like theirs would be to use the urban envrionments to their advantage. This was impossible in Ireland as the population was almost entirely hostile to their aim to destabilise the state, this in the vain hope of securing some advantage that might later present itself. As a result, a force that was estimated at being about two hundred and fifty strong infiltrated the Sliabh Bloom mountains, mostly staying in small groups of ten or less. More importantly, they were believed to have brought a disporportionate amount of weapons, ammunition explosives and other materials with them. The Sliabh Blooms was to be their redoubt from which they would launch attacks against the midlands towns in the same way that attacks by unionist and republican groups in the north were already escalating. Their aim by now was to essentially to make Ireland one country entirely at war. If this sounds like the goal of an increasingly desperate organisation that would be correct, but no one knew at that point just how short the road ahead of the IRA was. *Operation Garden Harvest* was intended to prevent the southern campaign of the IRA before it started and deal a critical blow to their ability to maintain operations along the border. In that it was successful.

Operation Garden Harvest (two weeks earlier)

Cpl Diane Keane

'Anyone who has done any kind of time in the Sliabh Blooms will tell you the same thing. It looks like it should be easy, but it isn't. Seriously, Naismith's rule telling you how long it should take you to walk a certain distance? That does *not* apply here. You just can't cover ground as quick as you think you will. Anyway, not the point right now. To give you the tourist book version, the Sliabh Blooms is the high point in the Midlands, which is largely flat. The bottom half, or more, is covered by commercial pine forests which are run through completely with walking trails and woodlands. It's quite nice if you're just out for a hike or mountain biking. The upper part is all blanket bog, there is no real peaks to speak of, just kind of one big flat plateau, running from the Ridge of Capard in the East and then sloping down in the West towards Kinnity in Offaly.

What this meant for us in taking the place back was, ok - the whole of the Midlands could be observed from there if you had a few OPs, a limited number of OPs in the right place staring out all over so every axis of advance towards the area could be observed. So not ideal in terms of sneaking up on anyone with any kind of numerical force worth talking about. But at the same time, this was as close as we were going to get to holding the IRA in a concentrated area where we could apply conventional tactics to it, force them to fight like we want to fight as opposed to playing the long game of guerrilla warfare. To do this, it meant that 2 Cav, which was already nominated as the national QRF, along with a battalion from Kilkenny who had become , you know, quite well practiced at mobile warfare at various different levels of intensity; they effectively surrounded the bottom part of the mountains. All the roads, in all the roads out were secured and cut off and they pushed in a little bit but then held position.

Now that was troops on the ground and probably if you look at the size of the area, you'll look at that number, 2 battalions effectively, and say that's not enough and you'd be right. With only that number in place the IRA could have just broken into smaller tiny units and just blended into the woods, into the valleys and a whole lot of them, even with all the ISR in the air, air they could find plenty of areas where they could just hideaway. And the fact that it matter is, you know, if you go back to late nineties, there was underground rifle ranges found in the Sliabh Blooms. It was an area that they themselves had *some* local knowledge of.

So, 2 Cav and friends surrounded the bottom of the mountains and that left the top. To prevent the IRA from being able to just sit tight or maybe slip through the holes in a tightening net of troops coming up from the bottom, the decision was made to put pressure on them from the top as well. In order to get enough troops in position as quickly as possible, techniques that were new to Ireland were employed.

All that is a fancy way of saying that I found myself in the back of a Casa CN235 with a static line hooked up running in low over the top of the blooms, jumping on to drop zones that had already been marked by Rangers who had inflated infiltrated the area by whatever means they always had for doing things invisibly. Apart from small scale use of paratroops in exercises, this was the first time that the Defence Forces ever really used an airborne force, and no one really knew how well it was going to pan out. So obviously with that three new, bigger, Casa aircraft that the Air Corps had bought, and the two older ones which were still kept in service once things went south, we had five aircraft in total trying to drop in hundreds of people who had previously done parachute courses over the years. If you think that the older Casa that I was on, which had been stripped out for transport, could only carry thirty five paratroops at a time, and the newer ones could carry forty eight, you can see that we weren't putting down a massive amount of people at one time, and multiple runs were going to be required. I mean, fortunately, it's a short way to Baldonnel by airplane, but that still left the turnaround time of about forty minutes between drops, at best. This time was filled in when multiple helicopters ran drops of troops who had prepositioned in smaller groups nearer to the area. It would've been harder to observe their build up this way. So, in first twenty minutes of airborne operations in Ireland, we managed to put around 260 troops on to the top of the mountain. From the five helis we had, they were bringing in about forty five, so call that platoon plus size number of troops at a time and they managed to get another forty five on quickly after the first drop. But we weren't going to have them forever they were needed back on the border, where it was expected that things would kick off there as soon as things kicked off in the Midlands too. But the Casas kept coming in and over the course of morning we managed to put just over six hundred airborne troops onto the top of the mountain, which was quite an impressive feat given that had never been done before, and especially as quite a few of them were first line reservists – exers who'd come back in for the fight.

Now, back to what I was saying about the Sliabh Blooms looking like it should be easy, but it isn't. Anyone who's walked up there will tell you, this blanket bog on the top of the Hill, well it sounds like a soft landing but it's really not what you want to be jumping into on round parachutes. Especially with all the kit we were carrying. There were multiple casualties on that first drop and all the subsequent ones as well, guys were simply sinking in and bending the wrong way in the bog when they landed. You could take your chances with a proper landing and sink into the bog, or at the last minute you could kind of curl up a bit and take a soft landing in the heather or, hey, maybe crack your head on a rock!

So, my job, or rather my sections job? At first it was just to secure a landing site for helicopters to come in and evacuate people. One heli had been held off just for that although it turned out that most of them were taking people off after the first wave. I was already down one person in my section, because Dave Lennon, he was my 2i/c, he landed and basically went up to his knees and rotated forward which broke both his legs. So, he was in a bad way and he was the first one that we actually evacuated from our dropzone. I think in total there were something like twenty-three guys injured badly enough to be taken off the hill, just from the drops alone, but apparently those figures are about right for what is expected on a parachute drop of that size.

Anyway, our job as a force at that point, was to essentially take control of the top of the mountains, deny the use of them to the IRA and in platoon size units start eliminating any forces that we came across in that area, and start driving down into the forestry. Obviously, platoon size movements split us up a little bit, but it was the biggest size of a unit that you could actually make work in the terrain we were fighting through. In some ways, this prevented us from using our conventional strength against the IRA but it was pretty much the right size for most of the groups that we did come across. There were only one or two areas where people came across bigger concentrations and those were dealt with by artillery and airstrikes. In fact, this was really the first major integrated use of close air support in Ireland as well. This came from Air Corps PC 9 training aircraft firing unguided rockets and 50 caliber machine guns. I'd have to say these were partially successful. I saw one or two strikes go in, but I didn't get call for one myself. From what the guys were telling me, the people who called them in, they were successful if they hit hard ground. If they were firing at the forests or onto a trackway that was fine, but in the bogs the weapons would just bury themselves into the ground. In some cases, they actually started forest fires, which were not unproductive for us,

I suppose. It definitely, well, you can't defend any position in a wooded area when it's on fire all around you, so it pushed the IRA onto the move, where they were easier to pick off. It wasn't a deliberate policy; you've heard some accusing us of 'ecological terrorism'. But I suppose that's Twitter for you.

It was a bit frustrating for us I suppose. The second wave came in. But those of us holding landing sites, our job was to stay there and start organising and getting the incoming troops, you know, set up and oriented and on their way to fight. But I suppose the thing was at that point, we were saying we wanted to do that too, I suppose the reason being, after all winter, it seemed like we were playing to our strengths now as opposed to theirs, and everyone wanted a piece of that.

The first day of the operation...So probably the biggest success, um, they say we accounted for half the IRA out there just on that first day, just by taking them by surprise. They were obviously expecting a ground intervention, but they had nowhere to go when we landed on top as well. The airborne troops effectively pushed a lot of them down into it waiting hands of 2 Cav, who were more than happy to pick them off. Most were captured alive and uninjured on that day, just purely true the shock and surprise factor from the way that we deployed. It was in the next few days done things inevitably ground down a little bit. From then on, we got to do our bit of patrolling after all, and yeah, we started to encounter guys digging trench systems, underground caches with spider holes for defence that hadn't been policed up on the first day. Over on the western end towards Kinnity, unfortunately, two of our guys from my Company were killed by snipers. That was taken care of pretty quickly with PC-9s. In that case the platoon was able to move in and recover bodies and weapons, proving that the airstrike had been successful.

And that was it for the next five days really, it was the old school section attack of style tactics just like in the Glen of Imaal. If you've ever tried to fight in those kinds of areas, like, the whole area, it's wood once you push down through the tree line. It's just blanketed with this thick carpet of pine needles, roots, it's dark in the middle of the day in there. Plenty of shade and shadow and contrast, all the things you need to hide and camouflage yourself, so yeah, in a lot of cases it was watch out for IEDs, watch out for trip wires, rifle barrels, anything regularly shaped that would give away a position And then assault that position with machine guns and grenades. Yeah, pretty old school. I mean a lot of what I learned coming up, it was based on the idea of having supporting arms and supporting weapon systems, but this sounds a whole lot more like when my mother told me what her recruit training was like. You weren't expecting to have anything to back you up, you just got on with it and that's what we did.

They reckon over the course of that five days, six days really when you include the drop, that we captured or killed as many as two hundred and twenty IRA members, with the rest either still bogging down in small positions in the Sliabh Blooms or escaping. That was to be expected. I mean, it's a mountain range: you're never going to seal off every single possible aspect and if people break up into smaller groups, then yeah, they're going to be able to get out. Critically though, they're not going to carry their heavy weapons, they're not going to carry their explosives and just hop on the bus in Portlaoise and head back North. That was seen as a really major success, but it did cost us eleven dead in the end, and about fifty seven injured in direct combat, so that's not including the parachute injuries. It was a heavy cost and, you know- people died in ones and twos during the Black Winter, but this - this I think was our first real exposure, and the public's first real exposure, to what it means to be at war in your own country. That there was a cost. Now, when the cost is nearly one hundred people who aren't going to be able to soldier anymore, or not for a long while anyway, that also was having a massive impact on the Defence Forces itself in terms of pure numbers. I was lucky. Dave Lennon was the only guy that I lost from my section injured. But one of the other platoons, Jesus. Of the eleven dead, three came from just one section with four more injured. Nearly a whole section wiped out. One guy triggered an IED which took out two of them. The rest were engaged by machine gunfire and the IRA guys that did it, they just bugged out. No one knows if those guys were subsequently caught in another engagement or if they actually escaped. It's frustrating.

But once the operation was done, you know, we spent another few weeks there before everything kicked off again in the Cooleys. And, of course, we had some of the new reserve guys come in. That's the second line guys, not the exers most of whom were retraining over the winter and getting back up to speed. These were the 'new FCA', a few guys from who'd been patrolling on the border for about a month at that stage, so still pretty fresh. They were actually a lot better than I would've thought. There was a resentment, at first, all that taking them out and holding their hands, but I think we all realised as well, that we had to build them up quickly and effectively if we were ever going to get any respite ourselves. And if we were going to put the bullet in the whole border campaign altogether. So, yeah, after the main operation was done, we spend just more weeks patrolling, patrolling, patrolling. Teaching, mentoring these new guys and then patrolling some more. God, what I would have given for cup of proper coffee in the middle of all that.'

CHAP 4

External Action 1

By the late start of spring 2021, the conversation on 'who' was supplying the groups in Northern Ireland had changed to 'how'. There was now little question that direct Russian support was being given to various factions. There was also little doubt that the desired end state was one of internal violence and war. The spillover into Ireland was not the priority, just a nice bonus from the point of view of the Kremlin. This pattern fit with previous Russian actions in Eastern Europe and it's cyberwarfare elements dovetailed almost exactly with it's efforts during the Brexit Campaign and the US presidential elections, to name the two most familiar to english speakers.

The pattern by now was clear – agitate civil unrest through online campaigns and the strategic application of pressure to key speakers, stoke these embers into violence, escalate that violence through the provision of material and sometimes barely clandestine military support and then de-escalate when the opportune moment presented itself and Russian interests were served. This didn't mean the violence would stop, just that it would return to a previous level that somehow felt less bad now, and which the international community would accept as the new status quo, thereby averting all out war. But Ireland was not the 'Near Abroad', not one of the countries on the periphery of old Tsarist and Soviet Empires that Russia saw as places where their own needs trumped the domestic ones.

There was no longstanding ethnic Russian minority that they could work through or intervene to 'protect', thereby forcing them to find other proxies.

Most crucially, however, there was no land border. You could not walk from Moscow, or even Kaliningrad to Ireland with a rifle on your back. You could not drive Buk surface to air missiles across a frontier and then deny their existence. Simply put, creating an insurection in Northern Ireland and then supporting it created logistical problems for Russia. Fortunately, from their perspective, patterns of behaviour had already been established that allowed them to move large shipments of weapons and ammunition onto the whole island with only a little sleight of hand. It appears that several different approaches were taken, depending on the phase of the war.

◆ ◆ ◆

Phase One – Nothing to see here.

This phase can be said to have run from sometime in 2019 to the start of the Black Winter. During this phase, supply efforts of materials was generally accomplished by sea. With the well publicised personnel problems of the Naval Service preventing thorough patrolling of the littoral domain, this was the lowest hanging fruit and the easiest way to move significant volumes quickly. It was also an easy way to move people off island without moving through airports during the initial Covid-19 crisis, but more of that later. The lack of available ships coupled with the Irish Air Corps having only two maritime patrol aircraft at the time, and the RAF none, all combined to provide the Russian state with a discrete and effective method of dealing with its logistical problems.

It is guessed that approximately half of all weapons supplied came ashore at this time, not in ports like Killybegs, but on the barren and remote strands and rocky beaches of Irelands most northerly county, Donegal. There is some tantalising evidence to suggest that a Kilo class submarine even entered Lough Swilly to either off load weapons or people, but this seems unlikely as a regular supply route and if it did happen, was probably a one off experiment given that drawing increased attention to submarine activity in that area, would by default have highlighted their operations around the sub sea fibre optic cabling south west of Kerry. In any case, once hostilities commenced and comparatively large numbers of sailors, aircrew and technicians re-entered the Defence Forces these coastlines became far more intensively patrolled during Operation Saltmine, the combined arms effort to prevent the landing of weapons in Ireland by sea.

Occuring simultaneously with this phase was the building up of proxy forces, including both dissident republican and unionist forces. Obviously, each group was trained unknown to the other. This involved the removal from Ireland, initially by normal commercial flights and later by sea of those people who had been either groomed and radicalised online, or who were volunteers from their respective community. The key ingredient in their selection was that they must never have come to the attention of the authorities before for any kind of sectarian or poilitically inspired activities. This was found to be more difficult than expected, based on reports from captured prisoners from both sides of the Northern Irish community.

This was because, as has previously been stated, there was no real support in each community for a return to violence. This meant that not only would the normal networks of safe houses, small arms dumps and information gathering not be available to them, but, to mangle an analogy of guerrilla warfare, these fish would be swimming in a shallow and hostile sea, not one disposed to their success. This lack of available personnel was so much of a problem, that it is now suspected, in some quarters, that the arming of the IRA was in part down to the fact that it was taking longer than expected to train a suitable number of future insurgents; and the clock on Brexit and its associated political tensions was ticking. They needed a dog in the fight and the IRA would do until their own pups grew up.

This fact, if it is indeed a fact, greatly influenced the future progression of the war. Instead of taking away an entire 'army' in one fell swoop for training, the Russians were forced to train each cohort of one hundred to two hundred people, and then rely on them to point towards who they believed would be suitable for the next training cohort. Republicans were enticed with the 'one last push' argument, that the chaos of Brexit would provide the clear path to a united Ireland, whilst unionists were recruited with the exact opposite position : arm up now or be over taken in the near future demographically and by a border poll. Critically however, each community in Northern Ireland had only a comparitively small and very much finite amount of people who were willing to take up arms against the wishes of their own people.

This carrying capacity, the amount of people predisposed to act this way that exists in any society, meant that the republican effort was already split – some of those who might have joined the Russian backed dissidents were already in action on the border with the IRA and were eventually lost to the republican side altogether.

These factors, a long but clandestine supply line, personnel invisible to the security services and a sectarian divide that was further split on the republican side heavily influenced the future path of the war that was so, so different than the Troubles. But that was yet to come.

Phase two – Air Superiority

This phase can be said to extend from the start of *Operation Salt-mine* in November 2020 and continue until the French truly got a handle on their QRA tasks in the Northwest. There were not smoothly defined breaks between phases and to some extent they may both be still ongoing. As Operation Saltmine ramped up its scrutiny on the Irish maritime domain on the backs of existing, new and returning Defence Forces personnel, it became clear that logistical resupply by surface vessel was increasingly likely to be detected. Fortunately for the Russian, dissident and unionist forces, when Brexit slams a door it opens a window. This window was the withdrawal of British air policing from Irish airspace during the Black Winter as the political impasse developed and grew worse. Intended to cause pressure on Ireland, it did, but ultimately proved to be an own goal as well. The French offer to replace the RAF came almost immediately, but the jets took longer.

Russia took advantage of this window to begin resupply by air. With no air defence assets available to the Air Corps, and with RAF jets no longer taking the hand off of incoming Russian aircraft from other NATO forces if the trajectory was towards Irelands West coast rather than Scotland, Russian transport aircraft began nocturnal drops of GPS (or rather GLONASS, the Russian sattelite based navigation system), guided parachute drops. Cheap and effective, these packages of up to a half tonne each were dropped under massive self steering rectangular parachutes from high altitude. The prevailing westerly winds did the rest, taking their deadly cargo to dropzones in both Ireland and Northern Ireland depending on the intended recipient. Not all got there however, some parachutes were recovered from the nets of Donegal fishing boats, but the most infamous was the one that tangled on the pinnacle of Mount Errigal in Donegal and spilled its load of small arms and rocket launchers down the steep sides of that mountain.

This method was able to succeed so quickly, so early because of the pattern of behaviour that had been built up over years of Russian long range aircraft flying down the west coast of Ireland without any more inconvenience than posing a danger to commercial traffic by not using their transponders to identify exactly where they were. Simply put, the wolf had scratched at the door and gone on its way so many times that no one thought it would ever bite.

During the start of this phase, the first constituted units of the new Northern groups, as opposed to the IRA, began to return home. They did not begin major operations however, with the exception of the fighting between the dissidents and the IRA for border access. There was still killing as each group bumped up against each other, but the worst was still ahead. It is uncertain at what point that each group realised that they had all been supplied by Russia, but many individual rubicons had been passed by then and they could not complain, less they be cut off from supplies and overwhelmed by their enemies.

Phase Three – Status Quo

Once the French QRA operating out of Shannon became established, the frequency of supply did not diminish, rather it blended modes and changed form from time to time. Rather than one or two transport aircraft that could easily be intercepted by the detachment, there might be a trail of successive flights of transports, maritime patrol aircraft and the occasional White Swan, a large intercontinental bomber. By swarming like this and moving through flight levels and airways that were used by commercial traffic, the Russians were able to absorb the available interceptors and prioritise where those jets went by posing an imminent threat to the safety of civilian air travel. This allowed them to continue airborne resupply missions, but with deniability now stretched wafer thin. This might happen day after day for a week, and then nothing for a month.

Equally during this phase, the ships and aircraft of *Operation Saltmine* saw an uptick in trawlers flagged in various states entering Irish waters. Effectively a similar technique was used here – an attempt to swarm the capacity of the available assets and then carry on with deliveries once they were saturated. Always assumed, but never proven without a proper sub sea monitoring capability, was that submarine activity was increasing as well. Again, the evidence was being provided by the fishermen of Killybegs, with the incidence of ships being mysteriously dragged by their nets or in one case almost overturned by submerged vessels going up all the time.

It is unclear at this time if this phase has come completely to a close.

Interlude: Red Team 'On the inapplicability of work group targetting in the current counter insurgency climate'

"Brendan" Red Team Member

'The joke in the DF was always that if we were ever attacked, we'd have to nuke Newbridge (where the DOD is located) on the first night and then turn to face the next enemy, because we were too small to fight a war on two fronts. There's some in the civil service who say we cajolled or threatened the staff that left when the Senator took over, but that's not true at all.

He directed that, as a somewhat outside agency in that we were all exers, we should do an analysis of the whole defence organisiation, our enemies as they existed at the time and provide a report on the strengths and weaknesses we observed. That of course included the civil side of the house in DFHQ. I think he just wanted more evidence for what he already knew.

To the surprise of some, we spent as much time on anthropological factors as we did on the tenets of guerilla warfare and counter insurgency force requirements. One thing that we leaned on was the existence of work groups - this is a brief overview, we actually conducted studies and surveys to prove our findings as well – and the cultures that existed within each work group.

What I mean by that is, that you could have a body of people who existed within a distinct working environment, for example, Infantry officers. They brought with them into HQ appointments an existing set of mental tools and a cultural prism through which they viewed the world. There were unwritten things that were acceptable and unacceptable to them, that might be different to another work group. These were things that were built, not just on their own personal experience, but of all those others who had come before them. Air Corps Commandants (Comdts) proved to be the hardest to pin down in this, by the way, and represented something of an outlier statistically.

This was because they were often working as squadron commanders, line pilots, instructors and staff officers all at the same time, so they belonged to all these different work groups and were hard to define. We found, with a bit of digging, that they would act in the same way as the group they personnally identified with most, rather than the one they were necessarily in. So if a pilot saw himself as a line pilot, he would act like that and be out of sync with his role as a HQ staff officer. But all that's an aside.

The real red light that came on was the acceptability of military failure amongst senior civil servants in the DOD, so long as bureaucratic process was followed and their own very strict control over entirely military responsibilties was maintained.

They were happy enough for capabilities to be lost through the personnel retention crisis, so long as they could squeeze the existing budget and try to bring in new, inexperienced, replacements. This, and it was very clear from the start, was not going to mesh well with the incoming ministerial drive to accelerate processes like recruitment and replenishment of equipment and the expansion of capabilities. Simply, there was a cultural divide that could not be crossed and those civil servants that left saw that and retired before they were nudged out to watch paint dry as the assistant secretary of bathroom refurbishment or whatever. We had recommended moves to change the culture that existed alright, but they upped and left before anything we suggested could be implemented.That was the sum total of our involvement, I just thought I should clear that up, as we get a very ominous reputation sometimes that is not entirely deserved!

We applied a similar analysis approach to the IRA, but without Survey monkey being trotted out of course! What we found was that they were actually harder to split up into groups, I mean , of course you had the cell structure etc – that was all dealt with under the counter insurgency heading of the report. No, what I'm saying is that culturally, you only really had two groups. These were the old command network that existed from the olden days and the new recruits. This second group, no matter what position of responsibility they were put in, they were still raw and inexperienced. Well trained, but not experienced.

This meant that for us to react to that, well, we couldn't go down the line of the NATO forces in Afghanistan or the Americans world wide where you target the middle management, the operational level officers who tie the whole thing together, because they weren't really there yet.

There was no super reliable experienced guy who a IRA commander could go to and say 'take these three cells and cooordinate an attack please without any of them knowing about each others role'. So their own old command structure was no longer familiar to themselves and they had to learn new tricks as well. While this affected their ability to fight, it also affected ours. If we couldn't cripple them by removing the operational level leaders because they didn't exist, then we had to beat them on the field. We went round and round with that one to find something better that might actually work, but we kept coming back to that as the only real option if we were to stop things getting out of hand, nationally.

Over the run of things during the whole winter of 2020, we were of course cogniscent of the existance of the other groups – you couldn't miss the killings going on in the North – but with the assets that we had as a country and the fact that these were new and developing groups, we really had no choice but to deal with the imminent threat first, and then see how things developed. And remember, all that up there should really have been the responsibility of the UK, but the policing only model was already under increasing strain, in the face of the firepower they were facing. Some in the media have said that we beat the IRA and all we achieved was to facilitate the new groups rise, but we had to defeat the near enemy first anyway. The others were just rising at the same time regardless of anything we could have done.'

CHAP 5

An Táin

With units sweeping in from the Northwest as well as the midlands (this being Finners 28 Bn and most of the force used to dislodge the IRA from the Sliabh Blooms) in order to try to defeat a force from Ulster in the Cooley Mountains, it was almost ineivitable that the operation to utterly destroy the IRAs' ability to make war on a large scale became known as An Tàin; after the semi-mythological raid by Queen Maedbh to seize the Black Bull of Cooley. Whereas that raids army fell largely by the sole work of Cuchulain, the modern Defence Forces fared much better. It is undoubted that much of the IRAs combat force had been spent in the Sliabh Blooms, but they had also been coming under increasing dissident pressure and police pressure in the North. If the midland mountain range was to be their means of spreading their campaign and taking pressure off themselves in the border, then their north eastern keep was to be in situated in the Cooleys. With it's back to water on three sides, occupying this range allowed them to monitor approaches and use such personnel as they had left to block access to the peninsula in Co Louth. Watching the IRA from the outside, the Defence Forces now essentially faced two options.

Reeling still from the shock of their catastrophe in the Sliabh Blooms, the IRA might split and factionalise. This would allow each weaker group to be picked off successfully but over a longer period of time. This relied however on *hoping* that the

IRA would split, *hoping* they could then be picked off easily or brought to surrender, *hoping* that not too many innocents would die in the waiting. Hope was in short supply however and enough, but by no means all, in power were beginning to see that things won't always work out the way you want, just because you'd like them to. This first option, did not have many supporters.

The second option was to continue the momentum of *Operation Garden Harvest* and attempt to deal a decisive blow, while the majority of the enemy were still on the Cooleys working out their own next move. Smaller area, fewer civilians at risk, a better chance of applying conventional tactics to the task. The downside of course, was that no operation of that scale would be able to go ahead without casualties, indeed, with the infamous destruction of Wolf 2, the Defence Forces would lose more people in one fell swoop than in any other single act of combat to date, including during the ambush at Niemba. The other downside was of course that the relieve effect of the the newly trained recruits, and the introduction of the first and second line reserves, was only beginning to be felt and did not yet have a universal effect.

The question was asked - did the troops of the old army have this one last push left in them, while still helping with securing the border? The opportunity was considered too good to pass up and the risks were accepted at the political and strategic levels. Compared to the intricate planning that went into *Garden Harvest*, time did not afford as much preperation. Nevertheless, Operation Swallow was given the go ahead. An Tàin - The Raid - was on.

Late April 2021

Cooley Mountains

Comdt Dave Heally

'The force coming out of the Sliabh Blooms, plus the combined efforts of the 28 battalion from Finner, plus as many of the people like ourselves that could be scraped off the border without completely leaving it open were pretty much what we had for Operation Swallow. The plan of course, was that we would essentially form a line, pretty simple really, form a line across the peninsula and then work our way through, all the way to the sea on the eastern side. We had the use of as many helicopters as the Air Corps could give us. This number had been just recently increased, actually, by the addition of several more AW139s, but this was before the Chinooks had arrived. So, in total I think we had something like eight AW139s available to us plus two smaller EC135's. The others were being held back to continue supporting the reserve efforts on the border, where things had been spread very thin to get this operation happening at all. We were worried about that to be honest.

As well as that, on the air side we had a PC-9s again. Four, I think, had been dedicated to us. I was less involved in that; I just knew they were going to be there with a CAP, that's a Combat Air Patrol set up for us. In addition to that of course we had the PC 12 Spectres, which were beginning to really make their presence felt as an ISR asset. They were gold for us in terms of identifying the layout of the IRA defences. We didn't have paratroops this time. As an organisation, we just did not have the time available to kind of really assess how it had gone in the Slaibh Blooms and ask ourselves what problems we had gotten away with initially that wouldn't work here. But to be honest that actually worked in our favor um, what the Spectres were able to tell us was that every place that looked like it could be a drop zone for anything upwards of a platoon, was being covered off by elements of the IRA. So, they had split their forces and they were in static positions. This of course was of great use to us. Some of these areas were, shall we say, thoroughly prepared by artillery; as a deception plan more or less, but also this is where the first hits were brought in on IRA personnel. So, between the combat air patrol, the helis, the artillery, our own drones it was pretty busy airspace over a small area. From what some of the Air Corps guys have been telling me, it was comparatively packed - we couldn't fit much more in there even if we did have it available, but yeah it worked quite well up to a point.

How we maneuvered through the area , what we essentially did was, through ISR, from the Spectres, through the use of the helicopters for direct recce, and the drones, and whatever else we had available to us, we began moving in usually platoon strength units on three or four 139s, which had their own machine guns and then also with the EC135s with snipers on board. Commanders like myself were on board the 135s and that provided a bird's eye view for us, to direct the ground movements of our troops. It worked very well, we were sitting beside the Air Corps Air Mission Commander, we were both looking at the same screen - a little flip down laptop in the back of the aircraft. That had our blue force tracker's as we call it so we had a common picture of what was happening and could coordinate between us instantly. Along with an ISR feed, to top it all off , we had a sniper sitting beside us for when we had to ,ah, not so much for our own protection but for taking out individuals who would escape outside the cordons we were sending in around them on the other aircraft..

By and large from the western side of peninsula and throughout the whole lot of the peninsula really, the IRA had not gathered and concentrated in numbers - they had learned that particularly well from this Sliabh Blooms. So, you were typically finding maybe maximum groups of five to ten. Their intention was to try and delay the movements of personnel through the area initially. Tracks, roads in, all the rest were layered with IEDS and covered with machinegun positions, that would obviously slow our efforts pushing in, increase casualties, cause problems with the whole thing that would give them time to come up with a plan.

How we got around that was that we began pushing in that way of course, with the ground troops 2 Cav, 28 battalion, all on the ground, but we were also leapfrogging and attacking each area, each group of IRA. And we weren't doing this you know in a straightline East West, or North to South. We were picking fights from the ISR picture, we would then send in 139s' following either an airstrike or artillery strike. Send 139s full of troops and they would land on and engage. The command helicopters, the 135s like the one I was working in, they would stay back, up higher, the platoons would then cordon off a particular group, engage them and either destroy or capture them. A lot of times, what happened was that the ground troops would flush the IRA into maneuvering away, and they would then be picked off by a sniper in the command machine or by the door gunners in the 139s themselves. In fact, the initial Lessons Learned afterwards said that the helicopters accounted for somewhere in the region of 70 to 80% of all casualties caused to the enemy. That's through direct close-in combat, not through artillery or airstrikes.

The progress through the Cooleys was slow for the armoured units. They did suffer the delays that were intended to be suffered by them from the IRA perspective. They did take casualties, but the whole fact was, this is where the main body of troops was coming. For all the action and attention that the airmobile elements got, the numbers needed meant that ground pounding was the only way to move in a suitable force strength. As they cleared the way, more troops, even some of the new reservists, were feeding behind so that no area was left clear for the IRA to reoccupy. The intention was that once an area was passed by, it was then patrolled into and then kept clear. This whole operation was to be 'The End', remember, once an area was cleared it was to be occupied and that took numbers.

Overall it took eight days. It was intense. From an airmobile perspective, we were throwing guys into four to five firefights a day. They'd go through these fights, cordon, engage, destroy, search all the way to the end and extract. Whatever they could take in terms of prisoners or material, load it up and then go back and be ready to go in again. And they did this day after day, after day, with no relief. There was no relief available at all. Everyone was pretty exhausted by the end. What happened towards the last stages was that we'd bunched up many of the remaining IRA. Those who hadn't surrendered, or who hadn't been taken out during combat, were all pushed onto the very eastern slope of the mountains. We were also beginning to see the first introduction of surface to air missiles into action towards the end of that week, with the first one being fired at a PC –9(*authors note: it was later found that these had been rushed into Northern Ireland by Russia in a direct response to the actions in the Sliabh Blooms*). These weapons forced the PC-9s to a much higher altitude, from which they couldn't provide the kind of really precise close air support that we needed. Had they come lower, they would have essentially just been killed - they had no flares or any of the other countermeasures that would have protected them from those kinds of missiles. The helicopters were just too integral however to operations, and kept on plugging by hugging the ground, using the terrain to either mask their approach to an area or sometimes following tight on the heels of artillery. Generally, they were taking the risk, I suppose, in order to make the mission happen. Of course, the consequences at the end were grim. These things only work until they don't.

Anyway, I was saying towards the end - from about day six on - the enemy were buttoned up on the eastern side of the mountains. There was some concern that they were going to escape around onto the coast road and break out. Our artillery was further back to the west and it was proving difficult to get a clear shot in to where we knew they were. On that kind of slope, even a near miss laterally would drop along way further down the hill and the guns were already at maximum range, bringing them much closer was considered a security risk, but I think people in HQ were so busy that they just didn't want to think about planning the move when they had other options available.

We knew they were gathered and dug in in a wooded area on the eastern side. The PC-9s, as I said had been largely held off by the SAM threat. We knew they had some of these missiles, but not many. They were protecting this main area, but they didn't have enough to basically give one to each rifleman, we weren't seeing them being employed like that as we fought through the last groups and they would have used them if they had them. But it all left us with a bit of a fire support problem.

Obviously, advancing into those woods we knew that we would be facing Sliabh Blooms times one million in terms of concentration of firepower, IEDs, everything really. They had no reason to leave anything on the sidelines now, so we were keen to soften them up a bit. This was one of those rare occasions where DFHQ were ahead of the facts on the ground I suppose! I believe the suggestion originally came from an Air Corps pilot who had been involved on a combined arms shoot with the Navy before, rather than from the Naval Service themselves. They were fully occupied with the weapons interdiction operations at sea at that stage. But yeah, from sunset of night seven, three naval service vessels- still remaining out of sight of the coast- opened fire with their main guns from a distance of about 17 kilometers.

Once the first rounds started going in, the ships essentially began to leapfrog each other, coming in closer with two firing and one moving at any given time. And in that way, they closed the distance and, you know, there was then the psychological effect in that. Anyone on that eastern side of the hill could see what was shooting at them then but could do nothing about it. And that's impressive, three ships opening fire on your small area and you know it's not going to stop anytime soon – the actual size of the round was smaller than an artillery round but the ships were apparently filled with ammo, with a more or less every rule of safety at sea sacrificed for extra firepower. Topping that off, any pause in the naval fire was filled in when the PC-9s returned. They stayed high, but in this case that was fine. They were firing with a full load of rockets at a time, saturating the area as opposed to going for precision. They said that each single aircraft was putting down the equivalent of a full artillery battery barrage which is not bad for a training plane.

While all this was happening, ground forces, air mobile forces, everyone else made that rush into the area and began assaulting through on the ground. It was straightforward infantry work from there: close with the enemy and destroy them. it worked; I think everyone was feeling it from the destruction of Wolf 2 the previous day, so yeah, it worked. Close with the enemy and destroy them.'

The battle that ended the IRA as a source of threat to the existence of peace on the island of Ireland seems to have progressed remarkably quickly to older observers, who compare it to the IRA of the Troubles who lasted for decades. This is to overlook the many differences between the organisation in these time periods. The IRA destroyed in the Cooleys was one that was being forced to fight in a manner entirely unsuited to itself, and in a way that suited the Defence Forces, who were able to bring conventional tactics to the field in a way which would have been impossible in a more urban setting. It also typified what was becoming the de facto policy of Defence Forces operations at the time, at both the tactical and operational levels : gain control of an area through overwhelming force and speed, occupy it to clear the area of any remaining fighters and then patrol into the area constantly to prevent any enemy from using the area again.

The first part of this process increasingly used airmobile – helicopter borne – troops as the Air Corps' number of helicopters itself began to increase with the introduction of extra AW139s. Referenced in this account is the purchase order that had been made for the much bigger Chinook helicopters which could drop into battle an entire platoon of troops using the same number of pilots and crew as an AW139. This order was almost suspended after the loss of Wolf 2 and the risk of losing so many people in one go became less theoretical and much more real. Nevertheless, with the lead time to train pilots and technicians being so long, the ability to move more people at once was undoubtedly required and with the addition of defensive aides – flare dispensers and infra red jammers to distract heat seeking missiles – the heavy lift helicopter order was continued.

The follow up part of the process, occupying and clearing an area depended mainly on mobile troops travelling in MOWAG Piranha armoured personnel carriers. These too were increasingly upgraded as the conflict progressed and their vulnerability to IEDS and rocket launchers became apparent. Simple measures such as bar armour – a metal frame designed to detonate incoming weapons warhead outside the hull rather than inside it could have saved lives in the Cooleys, with one vehicle and crew having been lost to an RPG that had been turned into an IED. It was buried into the top of an earth bank, on the side of a track leading into the hills and was detonated by remote command. The rocket struck the vehicle in the flank, penetrated its hull and killed the driver and commander. The fact that it would have been worse if the APC had been full of troops at the time was little consolation.

The last part of the process, the constant patrolling, now fell to the part-time soldiers of the second line reserve, initially from locally raised units but soon from units from all over the country. The risk was less, but not none. These troops would complete their four months of military training with an almost exclusive focus on this task, with most other sections of the training syllabus being stripped away or reduced significantly. Modular courses and on the job training produced the organic NCO cadres of these units over time, but they were still officered by regulars and for much of the time, Sgts and above were still regular soldiers too.

These smaller scale operations continued throughout the Spring and Summer of 2021 as death throes of the IRA continued and new threats began to emerge, but Operation Swallow was seen as a success, but a costly one – twenty more dead and sixty four wounded. If the offensives in the Sliabh Blooms and the Cooley Mountains marked the end of the Black Winter, the loss of Wolf 2 was perhaps it's parting shot. One last spasm of pain before it disappeared with the main threat posed by the IRA.

Operation Swallow – Day 7

Comdt Brian Rafferty AC, Ret'd

'The skipper on Wolf 2 that day, I'd flown with him so many times in the left seat, you know, back from where we thought was the start of everything, that first job on the border that started all this, and a long time before that too. Even after I got my command upgrade, sometimes two captains would end up getting scheduled together, and even then, I really enjoyed flying with him. So even though so many other people lost their life in that incident, in my head it always comes back to him.

I know that sounds a bit weird, but you go on with the friends you start with and when you lose one of them, it's a bigger deal. He was the one I knew most.

His copilot that day was a new guy, same cadet class as Denny, the chap that died in the EC135 in the same area a few months earlier, so there was that horrible irony there too. The other crew members, the two gunners, they were new as well. I had flown with one of them a couple of times but didn't know them as well as some of the older crew guys, but the skipper that day, he was that old thing, a buddy, comrade in arms, we fought together, flown together for a long time. Yeah. We were friends. None of those other things made a difference on the day who he was crewed with or anything else, I'm not saying if I was there it would've been different or any of that rubbish.

He was in the middle of a three ship flight, plenty of experienced crew on the other two aircraft as well. They were running in low on the southern side of the Cooleys. That that was thought to be safe by that stage; and most of that area had been cleared out over the week of fighting. So, he was in the middle of the formation and just doing what we had been doing, you know, just fighting into an area with a group of enemy in there, look - just doing what we had been doing.

I was actually on the ground back in Dundalk at the time, refueling. We had just come back from an assault ourselves, not far from the same area. Just a little bit further over the ridgeline on the northern side. So, we were on the ground when we heard the news.

Talking to the other guys in the flight, the leader didn't see anything until it was all over. The first aircraft- they were flying ahead of everything that happened. The guys in the third aircraft saw it all unfold. Even they will tell you that's probably a dramatic way of putting it, it was over very, very quickly.

What happened, appears to be, that one of the areas we had cleared but hadn't been able to patrol into yet, the IRA sent two missile teams out of what became their final basecamp on the eastern side, sent them out to get further along to the west and hit us. Our lads were down low, loose tactical formation- so a good space between each aircraft for exactly this kind of reason - and according to the guys in the aircraft behind them; the first thing they saw was the first missile hitting and the aircraft just fireballed. The second missile, it just flew into that fireball and detonated. It, it didn't change anything. Nothing extra was done that the first shot hadn't already achieved.

There were a four crew and nine troops on that machine. One of the guys in the back was a Sergeant Dan Morris, he'd actually been on the ground for, as we called it, the 'first mission of the war' as well, so he didn't make it the rest of the way through things either.

Forensically, after the investigation, what we found out was that the first missile hit the exhaust on the near side, just flew straight into it. The missile was fired almost level with them, they were down that low, so it just flew right into the exhaust.

That engine exploded and more or less pushed the gearbox forward and tipped it over into the cabin. At the same time the fuel tanks went off and the other engine also exploded, and this cooked off everything else in the cabin that was there. So, you're talking ammunition, grenades and at least one AT-4 Short Range Anti Armor Weapon that the troops were using for bunker busting in the ground fights. They reckon that blew apart the gearbox and that it did a lot of the other damage as well. It just cooked off straight into the main gearbox. Like those things are made of rock, I mean they're practically carved out of granite. Have you any idea to kind of force that it takes to destroy one of those things? And we just found bits, it completely ruptured. Gears, casing, everything. We just found bits of it all over the hill. The second missile just flew right into all that and exploded. Really after that, there wasn't a whole lot left of any individual person in the cabin. Or the cockpit. Look, that whole sequence sounds long, but it was more or less instantaneous.

And of course, no one could stop, you know? The show had to go on. We were so close to finishing things off with that operation. There was no scope for stopping, we couldn't take that pressure off, but oh my God, did everyone feel it.

 I sometimes think back now, we thought this was it. Clear out the Cooleys and the war was as good as over. Deal with the clean up ops and get back to reality. We thought this was the big, final fight that the whole thing would end on. Those guys died thinking they were near the end. But it only got worse, didn't it?'

◆ ◆ ◆

Interlude: Project Drift

Comdt Brian Rafferty AC Ret'd

' You have to give it to the spooks, they know the game alright, don't they? By all accounts; and again some of this is based on heresay and some is experience, the NSCC wanted their own U2 spy planes. They weren't for sale so they had to make do with something else. At the start, the National Security Coordination Centre wasn't meant to have any actual assets of their own, they were just meant to be a clearing house for intelligence coming from the Gardai and J2. They knew though, that if they wanted to really have the ability to grasp and control a situation quickly they needed to be able to directly task things themselves and they couldn't as it stood. They had to request extra resources from us or the guards be thrown at something, and usually the resources weren't there. From an oversight point of view, their spending was accounted for very carefully by the Public Accounts Committee (although not in public) as no one wants a new intelligence agency going rogue in year one, do they? Line by line, every item accounted for. Labour intensive work that for an accountant.

Now, reasonable expenditure was fine if you could justify it and thats where Project Drift comes in. What I've heard, is that it was buried in plain sight in the PR section of the budget. So the PR guy needs a Laptop – seems reasonable. Needs a phone – sounds about right. Needs a Canon DSLR – okay, that's normal. Needs a TST-14 (SL) – Well don't know what that is but it probably goes with the camera. Needs photo editing software – legit! And so on and so on. So an accountant looking through all that probably won't know that a TST-14 (SL), is a jet powered self launching glider. I mean, I didnt't know that and I fly for a living. Not so expensive that anyone will notice and so cheap to run that you don't have to worry about budgeting for fuel or maintenance costs that would attract any attention. And that was it, with a bit of clever accounting, Ireland's new intelligence clearing house got it's own operations section, and an airborne one at that.

You may well be thinking that a glider is a great idea for a bit of sport flying at the weekend, but that it has certain restrictions inherent in it's design for operational flying in Irish conditions. You'd be absolutely correct, but Project Drift was designed to fail so that they could buy something else legitimately. First though, it had to work well enough to be replacement worthy. That was the problem.

Initially, the kit onboard was exactly just that one Canon DSLR and an iPhone to remotely operate it. They cut a hole in the airframe underneath the pilot, mounted the camera in there and faired it over with a flat glass panel. They drew a rough 'X' marks the spot on the canopy with a marker for the pilot to aim in roughly the right direction and then another guy in the back would fine tune the shot with the iphone and click 'snap'. Very basic, but when they also mounted a go pro in there, they started to get some usable results. But it was a glider. The little retractable jet engine on board that made it self launching had enough fuel for about an hour and a half. That's more than fine if you want to take off, climb a little bit and then shut it down and glide for a while as a sport, but if you want to take off, cruise to an operational area and then remain there for a useful time and then get clear again, well... They were pushed into use as soon as they were purchased, initially with the PR guy – it was actually the public relations officers idea – as the pilot. I'll be straight up, that job we did in May 2020, none of us had any idea that after we all left the scene, this guy was orbiting away overhead for another few hours. One of the other assets there pinged him alright and reported it, but it was all quietly dealt with then.

Pretty soon, it was clear that these things were not up to Irish conditions – that's how I know so much about them, I was tasked one day with flying a team of ARW out to a field in Sligo, where this PR guy was sitting very sheepish beside his glider with no fuel and well short of where he intended to be. He'd been flying into a headwind in Donegal that was stronger than he expected, and any of us could've told him that would happen, he'd cranked up his engine again to stay in position over his target for longer and then ran out of juice when he was on the way back to his landing site.

So we're sitting there, the Rangers are securing the place, this guy is trying not to say much of anything but is also a little bit shook so he's saying too much at the same time. Anyway, this unmarked truck pulls up with a container on the back, another guy hops out and between this second guy and the pilot the glider is disassembled and lifted into the back of the truck with a small crane. And lo and behold, Project Drift got some wider attention than it wanted in DF circles. Now, the NSCC brazened this one out. They said the problem wasn't that they were using gliders, it was that they didn't have the proper powered aircraft for the job. The whole thing about 'why the hell were you using anything?' never got addressed in the climate of the time. The Air Corps got extra Spectres as a result, but the NSCC got their birds too. There's was a Grob 520NG. If you've never seen one, go to Shannon. Theres at least one there that gets airborne multiple times a day for 'Atlantic weather surveys'. They look for all the world like a PC-9 with very long wings and a *lot* of unusual pods and antennas hanging out of it. It takes off, heads west over the sea and then disappears. Once its clear of any primary radar, those are the ones everyone thinks of as 'radar', they send out waves which bounce off a plane and come back, once it's clear of them, it stops transponding and vanishes. I saw a glint off a canopy of something at altitude one day when we were up just across the border from Derry, and I'm convinced that's what I saw. I don't know who's flying it,it's not any current or ex Air Corps guys that I know, or if they are they're not telling.

Similarly, I did spot two MD500 helicopters coming across the border, North to South, a few miles ahead of us one morning just after dawn in Monaghan. They had to have been on NVG and they had to have been up to something funky, but I didn't get a clear look at them and I couldn't swear they belong to NSCC. The gliders are still going too, though, they took the cameras and the guy in back out of them and put in a bunch of radios instead. They use them for rebros – rebroadcasting for someone who's out radio range of whatever ground callsign they're trying to talk to. The planet gets in the way sometimes, so they bounce the signal off the gliders. Apparently they were quite succesful in the Sliabh Blooms, in that they didn't land where they weren't meant to and they didn't get in the way. I've seen them once or twice closer up to the North as well which begs the question, who are they rebroing for up there?'

CHAP 5

Simmer

The period between the end of April, and Operation Swallow, and the end of October 2021 became known in Defence Forces parlance as 'The Simmer'. Unlike the Black Winter, this phrase did not enter public use to the same extent. It appeared, after everything that had happened, that things would return to normal. A newer and more generally effective vaccine was being promised to be available within months with the hint existed that going away for a Summer holiday in Europe might be back on the cards again. The public deserved a boost after the horrors of 2020 and early 2021 and the national mood was high. The Defence Forces mood, not so much.

The army that marched off the Cooleys, buried their dead and went back to work on the border was not the same force that existed a year before in 2020. Young soldiers who had less than a year in service, and who had never set foot in Lebanon, Mali or Syria were now combat veterans. Similarly, the force of the second line reserve, a supposed part time organisation, had a large number of it's soldiers working on a full time basis as civilian employment levels had not returned to pre Covid-19 levels yet. They needed them too, as the initial surge of recruits tapered off to just above replacement levels and the force never got close to it's establishment of twenty thousand. This would have been needed to fulfill the goal of one thousand reserve troops on the border each day, with no one needed there more than once every six weeks, while still allowing for training etc. These troops too, were hardening in the environment of constant tension that still existed for soldiers and Gardai at the EU's land border with the UK.

Brexit fuelled these tensions (with some online Russian assistance still forthcoming). If the public relationship between Irish and UK civilians was undamaged, the political relationship was under increasing strain. Senator Davis recounted that one member of the Government talked of ' the good old days when Priti Patel wanted to starve us to the negotiating table'. The relationship between the UK and the EU was pulled so tightly it was close to breaking point, as trade and defence negotiations continued against a backdrop of increasing sectarian violence in Northern Ireland.

From the start, the Irish Government had levied the removal of Ireland's territorial claim over Northern Ireland in the Good Friday Agreement, voted in by the majority of people on the island, as a way of insiting that the emergence of violence was not an 'Irish Problem' or ' The Troubles II', but a Brexit problem that now put a large number of EU citizens at threat. These being the Irish passport holders in Northern Ireland, which as Brexit took its toll on travel rights and the economy, now included a significant percentage of people who were and would always remain unionists.

Brussels took it's lead from Dublin on this matter and proceeded accordingly. Initially intended as a way of saying to the UK, 'we don't want any part of this violence, this is not of our doing', the message was instead taken up as EU interference in an internal matter for the UK. Initial offers of a EU force to assist in preventing further destabilisation, as a sign of solidarity, were loudly rebuffed. Any requests made by Brussels to the UN for peacekeepers were going to be vetoed by Britain, who had that power via a permanent seat on the UN Security Council, so they weren't made. Indeed, if the Black Winter was know for its biting cold, the Summer of 2021 was hot, close and politically febrile.

Except for those in the purist form of denial, all involved could see that things would come to a head soon. The build up of numbers in the Defence Forces continued, with veterans of the Slaibh Blooms and the Cooleys now joining the returning ex members of the Defence Forces in the training schools. These former members had been doing most of the recruit and skills training until then. Ammunition stores were replenished, controversial purchases such as the twin rotor Chinook helicopters arrived in country and conversion training began in earnest for crews and technicians.

As the reserves patrolled the border, the regular forces drove hard to recover their numbers, with all eyes to the north as the situation there worsened. On the 12th of July, the first direct assault by unionist forces on a republican civilian area took place with fifteen dead and two thousand made homeless. A reprisal attack the next day by the new dissident groups killed eleven unionist civilians and burned sixty houses. After a week of heavy fighting, the PSNI with the first, barely under the radar, signs of direct military support from the BA units stationed in Northern Ireland brought the situation under control. Things returned to the lower level of violence that had once again become normal. Then, on the 28 October 2021, the first rockets fell on Starfort 1.

Senator Ian Davis

' We all saw what was happening in Northern Ireland over those few months and knew we weren't done yet, even if that hadn't sunk in publicly. On the face of it, there was squabbling in the media between politicians from Ireland, the UK, and then also from Brussels, as the situation worsened and the offer of an

EU led stabilisation force was made. That situation, well the offer was genuine, but things weren't that straight forward. The relationship between the Gardai and the PSNI remained solid throughout the whole conflict, and through those channels we learned that the US had already made an offer to the UK of a similar force, which they had turned down.

Apart from the optics of it all, you must remember that the US at this stage was still going through it's own dark night of the soul after the violence during the 2020 election, with militias firing on lines of voters in predominantly democratic party areas, and the subsequent further deaths in the riots and 'policing' that followed. Regardless of the result of that election, which itself dragged on for some weeks, they were a divided nation and no one wanted to be the foreign war that unified them. That was, of course, the standard historical ploy of empires suffering domestic issues. Having turned down that offer, the UK could not accept one from the EU even if they had been of a mind to, which is admittedly unlikely.

Mistakes were being made politically south of the border as well, it must be said. There was a low but consistent stream of politicians and commentators reacting to the online drive for a border poll based on demographics, increasing unionist uptake of Irish passports and the benefits of EU membership. The security implications were never thought out by these commentators.

As the sectarian fighting escalated and temporarily peaked in July, I personnally cannot help but wonder if we, as a country, played a part in fuelling the fears of the Unionist groups through this political positioning. Ultimately we may have helped persuade those members of the Unionist groups, who would have been considered more moderate, to row in behind the Carsonite faction rather than split with it. I was keen that my Dail colleagues would express themselves with tact and moderation, that they should follow their believes but be aware of the wider audience they were transmitting to. Regretably, many thought that only their own constituency could hear them.

Even as the death toll began to rise amongst police seconded in from the UK, who appeared to be the primary target of the republican dissidents rather than the PSNI, the UK govt remained committed to not putting extra troops on the streets of NI. Note that 'extra' is more than none. About this time, we did see more of the British Army units that were homebased in the North occupying and defending key infrastructure, such as Stormont, and providing more covert support to the police as well. Their numbers precluded any decisive action however. They too began to suffer casualties, with one EOD team suffering one dead and two wounded during a routine counter IED mission that turned into an ambush, and also losing two of their Britten Norman Islander ISR aircraft to surface to air missiles. One to republicans and one to unionists.

The fight in the North was becoming increasingly intense and dangerous for all involved, as the Republican and Unionist factions fought each other in both urban and rural settings, with the bodycount of innocent civilians also increasing.

A notable change from previous times was that the forces remained largely mobile. Unlike during the Troubles, they did not have the community support to cache weapons and people continuosly in urban areas from their own co religionist background, and this applied to both sides. In the modern era, someone recording a paramilitary group storing weapons somewhere can share that video online; and it is further shared a thousand times before the police see it – the sheer scale and volume of possible online informants meant that it was more or less impossible for a group to track down an informant from their community and silence them.

This led to their habit of staying in larger, mobile, semi conventional groups, with both sides being willing to use their SAMS to protect the nature of their movements. With regards to the direct fighting between the groups, the style of combat came to resemble the Toyota Wars of Africa, but with the terrain dictating that the combatants usually had to dismount from their vehicles to fight. This lead to engagements where it was easy to flank and hard to withdraw once you were committed. Typically, encounters were resolved decisively with few on a losing side breaking contact succesfully.

As the fighting progressed, both sides also began to suffer from attrition that they could not easily afford. It wasn't major numbers at first but the writing was on the wall. As they began to clash in greater strength, the unionist side began to prevail. This was a weight of numbers issue – they both had the same training and equipment, but the Dissidents had already shared the available, recruitable bodies with the IRA which was now, if not wiped out, massively reduced.

This meant that in the warfare that developed, the unionist side was able to either apply more people to straight on assaults, they could use manouvre elements that were not available to republicans to bring confrontations to a close, if a fight became protracted they could rest their troops while the dissidents became physically exhausted and eventually overcome. Remember also, there was no taking prisioners in this fight. If you were in a battle, you won, escaped or died. It is reckoned that by the end of July, from a strength of about one thousand at the start of the fighting, the unionist side were down to approximately seven hundred and fifty to eight hundred. The Dissident side were down to about two hundred and fity from five hundred.

Weight of numbers would have suggested that the conflict would soon be resolved all other things being equal. But... Other voices were also being heard. The Scottish independence movement was a source of alarm for the unionists. As much as anything else, it is believed that this pushed them in a more radical direction, as an independent Scotland would only accelerate calls for a referendum on a United Ireland. Having seen the fear, and local demographic change, caused by the 'one off pogroms' in July, a faction in the unionist groups began to advocate for the 'removal of the nationalist voice from the ballot box by force' and to use violence to compel an increase to the British Army presence in Northern Ireland. This, in their mind, would solidify the Union between Britain and the North. This became the dominant voice in the unionist group.

In the same way as the republican groups were now referred to as Dissidents in order to put a distance between them and the community that rejected them but which they proposed to represent, this new faction were no longer called Unionists but Carsonites, named after Lord Edward Carson. Carson was the first signatory of the Ulster Covenant to resist Home Rule for Ireland in the early 1900s and founder of the Ulster Volunteers, the first Unionist paramilitary group. The nomenclature thus described became the standard internationally and further drew a line between this war and the Troubles.

The Carsonites also attempted to domestically replace their losses. While no one was interested in a sectarian fight against their neighbours, just like the IRA previously, they needed a campaign to serve as a recruitment banner. This is where the uptick in attacks on the border forts on our side began again, but civilian targets in Ireland were not yet getting the attention they were in the North.

For our own measure, we trained and equipped as many personnel as we could as quickly as we could, and in all disciplines. Those few months were a blessing for us really. We rested the regulars as much as we could, which wasn't much, and were able to concentrate the operational experience of the second line reservists. What the future would bring was at that point still unkown, but by precedence we knew it would not be good. The summer of 2021 was defined for us by force building, patrolling, interdicting weapons and a very anxious wait.'

CHAP 6

It all falls apart

Fuck Scotland. Fuck their independence.Fuck the Dissidents. Fuck the Carsonites. Fuck the Government. Fuck DFHQ. Fuck everyone, basically, who had put him back on this mountain again. Comdt Dave Heally had twisted his ankle. Swallowing his internal tirade, he listened as the second of his two forward platoons called in the possible contact that they were investigating. He was working his way through the Cooleys again, further west this time, almost beside the N1 Dublin – Belfast road but higher up on the slopes looking down on Dromod.

He was moving two up, two platoons forward, one to the rear and his HQ in the middle. His third platoon was a little shy, only about twenty people and while his first platoon was led by Lt Brian Quinlan, his second and third platoon were led by two fresh 2Lts who were straight out of their Platoon Commanders Battle Course. Trained but inexperienced and Quinlan, who he was soon losing to a Captain's staff position in DFHQ, his back injury having finally caught up with him, He'd love to say that he had a twenty year Platoon Sergeant to flesh out the knowledge levels in the two weaker platoons but that wasn't true either. NCO experience was becoming as thin on the ground as officers, as the army continued to grow. Although, he supposed that a year's worth of experience now, would go a long way. He had plenty of veterans of the fighting in the Sliabh Blooms and the Cooleys in his ranks, so that was something.

He wiped his face with the back of his hand as he listened to them advance to what turned out to not be a contact after all, just some fake IED that someone had left in place, up near the stone marker that marked the spot height on top of the flattening hill. He ordered them to stay away from it over the radio and recce the area further. He put his other two platoons to ground, and told them to cover off as the hairs rose on the back of his neck. Something about the whole set up felt wrong.

Had he been further up the hill, alongside the unfortunate 2 Platoon, he might have seen the flashes coming off the Mourne Mountains on the northern side of Carlingford Lough, the glacial fjord that seperated north from south here. In reality, they would probably have been hidden by the low cloud base that hung over the area. Either way, there would have been very little time to do anything except tell 2 Platoon to hit the ground like the rest of them. As the volley of rockets piled into the area around the stone marker, any number of things happened simultaneously for Dave Healy. He realised that they'd been drawn out to a prepared killing ground by the Carsonite cell firing the rockets, based on the supply of suspicious intelligence. He recommenced his internal tirade against the world in general for putting him in this situation. As the last explosion echoed away to nothing, he heard the screams twice, over the radio and from up the hill. And, like had become commonplace over the last year, he called it in and requested air and artillery support that wouldn't be allowed hit targets in the North anyway.

Still at risk of being fired on with a second volley, he had 1 Platoon gather the survivors of their stricken comrades and fall back down the hill, while 3 Platoon began to prepare landing sites for the ineivitable medevac helis. He looked up at the grey sky and cursed the whole world one more time, before getting down to the grim business of accounting for everyone in a platoon that had ceased to exist in a matter of seconds.

It was raining.

Comdt Dave Heally,

Nov 2021

' Do you know what a Grad rocket system is? Most of the time you tell people rocket attacks and they have no frame of reference between an RPG blowing up one vehicle and a Saturn 5 sending someone to the moon. The Grads were big 122mm rocket artillery. In their original format, they came in big multiple laucher tubes on the back of a truck, like someone had tied a bunch of drainpipes together and put them on a tripod. They'd fire in a volley and the newer rockets had a range of up to 52km, but they never went that far here. Plenty of targets closer in I suppose.

They were being airdropped in, we knew that by now, but obviously they had to travel a bit further that way so the launch vehicle was deleted from the package. I mean, you can airdrop the whole thing, truck and everything, but the vector is pretty much vertical, they wont go far. So what we ended up seeing, was that they had been dropped in in sets of eight tubes which were then locally mounted on trailers and towed to a launch site. Sometimes, and some of this is based on what we heard from the PSNI. Sometimes, these attacks would coincide with a bigger assault into an area and sometimes it was a hit and run. They'd just drive in at night, fire, pack up and be gone withing a few minutes.

At first, they were attacking fixed targets like the first strike on Starfort One. But by this time, thankfully, the Starforts were being abandoned anyway and the new border barracks were coming online. These might look green and nice and grassy, but that's just the dirt layer on top of all the buildings making things look pretty. Under that, it's all concrete and steel, they're proper hardened facilities designed for a long term fight. So, blowing up the old Starforts was fine, but they couldn't put much of a dent in the new barracks except to ruin the landscaping on the COs' flower garden.

They didn't stop hitting the fixed targets after that – I mean, how many times has the hydro electric plant in Ballyshannon been hit now? They did though put more thought into getting bang for their buck by hitting us on the move, be it in vehicles or on foot. People used to give the Mowags shit for being designed to take a hit from on top rather than the bottom, but we were glad of it when those bastards started dropping around us, I'll tell you that for nothing. This meant moving more and more by helicopter when we could, the SAM threat hadn't gone away but it was still something that could be tactically worked around most days.

My Company. Some days they were lucky, some days we were. That day, the Carsonites were lucky and good. They sent some dodgy int into the system, we responded in strength because you never knew if you would still come upon some rump IRA cell still trying to move some cache off the Cooleys. They'd obviously been watching how we respond to things. Anyway, they got us to a flattish part of the mountain where they would have the most effect and ... They were airburst weapons that day. If it had been straight forward impact fused hi – ex they might have buried in the ground more before going off, saved a few people. That was the first big hit that the DF took in the second war, the Carsonite war. Had to be someone I suppose and we just got to be the ones to go down in history. Eight dead straight away, another six over the next few weeks in hospital and seventeen injured. The whole platoon gone in an instant, cos the injuries they took... None of that gang will soldier actively again, if at all in any capacity.

Now, the thing with the rocket attacks. Some things like, rifles, machine guns, even up to the SAMS and the mortars, you can kind of train someone and just let them rip, you know, even without much guidance they'll have a reasonable effect overall. The rockets are different, there's a reason that an artillery officers course is the most expensive in the Defence Forces and it's the same for those guys shooting at us.

There's no doubt in anyones mind that there were Russian advisors on the ground with them in small numbers, helping them plan and carry out the rocket attacks, whatever about any of the rest of it. And we weren't allowed hit back, no counter battery artillery or airstrikes. Part of that was because it was in the North and the UK would go balistic if we did some heavy bombardment on the place. The other part, I think , was they didn't want the political can of worms opened if you killed a few Russian artillery Spetsnaz who happened to be birdwatching in the North next to a BM 21 Grad launcher.

So this went on all winter and then suddenly tailored off and stopped. They didn't run out of rockets, they continued using them in the North and as IEDs, big ones. But they stopped the cross border attacks. We all figure someone started taking out the help, but never knew who. There was enough going on to keep us occupied anyway.'

Senator Ian Davis

'The movement for Scottish independence had reemerged as a growing force ever since the Brexit referendum, but had become stronger again in the year following the UKs actual exit from the EU. While we laboured through the Black Winter, in Scotland, moves had been made to prepare the political ground for another independence vote in 2021. When Whitehall made it clear that this would not be allowed to happen, the devolved

Scottish parliament had debated the issue, and at the end of Spring 2021, announced that they would organise an 'indicative vote'.

This was cheekily playing with the term used in Westminister to assess what courses of action that parliament would support during the initial phases of Brexit some years ago. Essentially, this would be an Independence Referendum that wasn't. It was a way for the Scottish Parliament to say 'this is what our people want'. And of course it would go the way of the independence vote, because predictably, those in favour would come out to represent their interests. Those opposed stayed at home to boycott what they saw as a PR stunt. The margins were not small. 78% of those who voted , voted for independence. This lead to a summer of debate both in the media and in politics as to what this vote might actually mean. All of this played out against a backdrop of fighting in Northern Ireland – the fear factor being left unsaid was that 'this is where things go if you don't listen to people'. At the end of August, Westminister drew a line in the sand and said, again, that it would not permit a legitimate Independence referendum to be held.

The Scottish Independence movement saw this as a suppresion of their democratically expressed wishes and protested throughout the winter of 2021. Almost all were peaceful, but in every society there are those that will hijack such occasions for their own use. During a minority of protests some looting did take place, and small riots broke out. During one of these riots, a protestor found herself in the wrong place at the wrong time and was hit by a police van. She was innocent of any wrong doing, but the police that dismounted did not immediately help her, but tackled the riot instead. Her death may have been ineivitable, given her injuries. And the fact that the police said they needed to secure the area before helping was not entirely unreasonable, but the fact was, she died on camera. CCTV from a supermarket across the road saw her lying there for fifteen minutes before anyone offered assistance.

With it's first martyr, the independence drive accelerated. With all the talk of independence and seccesion from the Union, the Scottish Problem, as it became known in the UK, fed back directly and powerfully into the Carsonite psyche.'

Interlude: What's in a name?

March 2022.

Lt Jeanne 'Costa' Delaney

'The name Costa? That's Rover's fault. Actually, that's not entirely true. We were still Cadets so we were all idiots in the ways of the world. Rover's just stuck with that as a life plan longer than most. No, we all wanted cool sounding personal callsigns, just like the movies. (*Authors note: Lt Delaney is facepalming and clearly embarassed by this*). The boss, Comdt Mulvey, said this was fine but that he had the final call on each name. He knew what he was doing, everyone in the Defence Forces has a nickname and none of them are complimentary. Anyone who thought they were going to be called Maverick was in for a disappointment.

Anyway, in the tv series Battlestar Galactica, the female fighter pilot was called Starbuck. I thought this was definitely something I could live with when it was suggested, by Rover of course, but the boss instantly shot it down and came back with Costa. So since then and presumably until the day I die, I will be putting up with jokes about cappucinos, suggestions about giant coffee cup Halloween costumes and someone recently drunkenly told my fiance that when we get married he couldn't change *that* name. Yeah, that was Rover too.

Ask him about his name. He's got a few good stories about it, but the truth is, when we initially flew into Stockholm, he sat beside the boss. We asked him, the Comdt, how his flight was when we landed, you know, basic nervous cadet shit talk around a senior officer and he said it was 'like sitting next to a yelping labrador puppy for the whole fucking flight' and then stalked off to the baggage area. So regardless of what he tells ya, thats where 'Rover' came from.

For us, I guess we missed most of the war and everything that went with it. We were away from 2020 on, and not just away we were on an intense course of academics and flying. We stayed in touch with family and friends of course, and we got home for Denny Ratigans funeral for a few days, but we were really immersed in our own little world. We had flown PC – 9s at home to solo stage and instrument flying stage but before we went further than that, we were scooted off to Sweden for the SK60 Lead in Fighter course. The SK60 is a side by side jet trainer that they use before going onto fly fighters, they actually do their basic course on it too. We were one of the last classes to fly it, they'll go straight from basic to Gripens now, which will suit the Air Corps group that are on the basic course now. When we went out, the plan was that we would do the LIFT, Lead In Fighter Training, course and then conversion and operational training on the Gripen.

We're only doing the air to air stage of the course, the next few classes will do the multirole stuff, ground attack and recconnasiance, that kind of thing and we'll do it in modules at home. But the whole point is to have an interceptor capability for air policing and I think they want at least some of us back before the French get sick of it and pull out. A bit of overlap means we'll get to fly with them in mixed formations for a while to learn a bit more from their experience. At least that's the plan for now anyway.'

No 2 Operations Wing had previously operated Cessna aircraft from Gormanston before both the wing and Gormanston aerodrome itself were shuttered. Reactivated to take in the Gripen fighters that had been leased, it would soon be headquartered and based in Baldonnel with a permanent QRA detachment in Shannon. Similar to the other Wings, there was an operational Squadron – 201, a planned second squadron – 202 be based in Shannon, and a squadron of technicians and engineers 203 Sqaudron, along with the Wing HQ. The new wing and it's staff had spent the better part of two years training in Sweden to make the re-introduction of fighter jets, the first since the Vampires (the Fouga Magisters that replaced them were training aircraft), a success. While they would certainly be busy with the air policing role they expected, it was in an entirely different type battle that they would make Irish history with the first Irish Air Corps combat action against ground forces since the Civil War.

QRA: Unhappy coincidences

May 2022

100 miles West of Galway

Lt Col Christian eased back on the single throttle lever that controlled both engines on his Rafale fighter jet and slipped backwards relative to the KC 135 tanker he was refuelling from. As he disconnected, he considered that his quarry today dated from the same bygone era as the flying petrol station keeping him topped up. With a quick hand wave at his wingman who was disconnecting from the hose on the other wing of the old airliner turned tanker, he brought his aircraft around to the west and throttled up again. It wasn't like the Bear would out run him, but the longer he could annoy them the better.

The Irish detachment had not been bad for his squadron, it was already set up when they arrived two months ago on their second rotation, most of his pilots had been here before already. That meant it was a nice easy work up for the new ones, finding their way in a real operation for the first time. And real it certainly was. Whereas QRA in France might launch occasionally for a stray airliner who'd lost radio contact, here they were airborne almost every shift dealing with Russian incursions.

They typically came in three types, one was the cargo aircraft snooping around the northwest to drop arms when they got the chance, the second was 'routine' Russian ops – the normal runs through the Atlantic that they made to test NATOs; and now Ireland's, QRA response. Today was almost certainly the third kind. A TU 142 Bear F. A coldwar relic that was still a very capable maritime patrol aircraft. The TU 142 was modeled on the TU 95 Bear bomber, which was itself derived from the TU 4 Bull – a rivet for rivet copy of the American B 29 that bombed Hirsohima and Nagasaki. So its lineage was distinguished, but these days it was serving a very different purpose. Marpat – maritime patrol.

In these days of 'everyone knows but no one can prove it' shadow play, the Bears were marpatting for the fleet of civilian registered Russian trawlers that were feeding weapons into the war in Ireland; whenever the attention on airdrops came too close to the bubbling over into a realworld problem. They would fly down the coast as far as South West of Kerry, swing around and head back up again. All the time, the were constantly scanning and sweeping electronically for any naval vessels, be they Irish, UK or EU that might interfere with their landing operations. This one was on the way back North. They were taking over from the previous flight of Rafales that had launched to intercept over an hour ago. Even with three external fuel tanks they were sucking gas at a prodigous rate to close the distance and the tanker took off from Shannon soon after the first wave. Lt Col Christians' jets had overhauled the tanker at a leisurely fuel conserving rate, and had just topped up the tanks to allow them to stay with the Bear for as long as they could. The first wave would be thirsty by now, so he came up on the squadron chat frequency for a handover.

"Bonsoir chief, one Bear F as advertised, on my squawk, heading 010 degrees, 380kts FL 300. He's trailing a comms antennae so keep clear across his six.' He responded to the first waves update with two clicks of his own radio, no point giving away more than you had to, when the Russians were undoubtedly trying to listen, encryption or not. The message had told him the big turboprop was being formated on by the first wave and he should track their transpdonder for the location as the Bear didn't have his switched on. This saved him turning on his radar, more electrons saved from observation. The rest told him the Bear was heading just east of north at 380 nautical miles an hour at 30,000 feet. The remark about the comms antennae told him that the Russians were trailing a long cable used to communicate with submarines, for several kilometres behind him. At this height and speed, that was more about pissing off the French pilots who had to avoid a nearly invisible wire saw in the sky, rather than any real attempt at communicating with anyone.

Tracking his squadron mates on the head up display on top of his instrument panel, the 'friendly' signal of the distant Rafale in front of him was soon joined by a box with a small but growing dot in the centre. His jet had picked up the heat of the Russian airplanes' exhaust and was guiding him towards it. As the sun sat low on the western horizon to his left, he pulled up in formation with the big silver winged dinosaur and waved away his comrades who eagerly headed for the tanker. He closed the distance slowly, and once in posi-

tion, he could actully hear the other aircraft over the noise of his own twin jet engines. Shifting in his seat to get comfortable for the next hour or so, he sighed to himself. Another day at the office.

This comparative peace lasted for only twenty minutes, when the Bear swung to the West and descended rapidly. Wondering if the big machine had some kind of problem, he dodged the swirling cable that was now reeling in fast, and left his wingman high to relay comms if the Bear went all the way down to low level. He kept one eye on his fuel burn. The massive Bear had fuel for stooging around at low level, but he'd need the tanker again if he hung around in the dense lower air too long. Opening up the distance, he turned his own radar on air to surface mode but picked up the focus of the Russians attention visually almost at the same time.

An aircraft carrier, definitely worth descending for a look if you're a Russian navy maritime patrol crew. As he got closer, still in formation with the Bear, he could make out the two islands sticking above the flight deck that marked it out as a British Queen Elizabeth class boat. As the Russian levelled out and he began to think about his next course of action, out of the corner of his eye, Lt Col Christian picked up movement on the other side of the Tupolev. The silhouette against the dying sun was an F 35, no doubt the stealthy fighter had just launched from the big ship to intercept the Bear themselves. A thought occured, and looking over his shoulder, he spied another black sihouette sliding into position in his six o'clock high. "Well" he thought. " This is new."

Interlude: Boiling over.

Advanced Paramedic Shane Kelly was hungover, and the heat and humidity was not helping. It had, however, been totally worth it. It was the first get together for a long time. Ostensibly, it was a Clinical

Governance day where doctors, National Ambulance Service managers and both air and ground based frontline ambulance crews all met to discuss outstanding issues. Some staffing points were trashed out but as always, the best bit was listening to case studies, with this year's subject being the increase in trauma jobs. That much had gone well, it was a big deal with them not having really had a chance to sit down and take stock of things since... He couldn't remember the last time actually.

What had gone even better was the night out. With vaccine uptake in the general population increasing, and all frontline health staff having received their dose, restrictions were lifted a little and they had been able to properly let their hair down. He thought he'd been holding his own fairly well until Alan handed him a pint at three am. And then dropped a shot of Jagermeister into it. He hadn't remembered much after that. He stayed / passed out on Jerry and Anne's couch but was now on his way home. He got breakfast in town (a coffee and a quickly abandoned half eaten croissant, anything else was going to be ambitious) and was walking towards the Luas stop on Abbey Street to start making his way to the park and ride at the Red Cow to get his car. He might need another coffee before he hit the road, he figured.

His phone vibrated in his pocket as he got walked out of the supermarket beside the Abbey Street stop, second coffee in hand and his stomach complaining the whole time. He paused to shove a bottle of water in his small overnight bag and looked at the screen, two missed calls and a bunch of whatsapps from the boss. He knew things had been a bit blurry last night, but he didn't think he'd said anything out of order. He was beginning to scroll through the messages when the tram arrived.

Stepping onboard, he pushed through the thick rubber matting that now hung between carriages, smelling mildly of citrus disinfectant. These had been introduced late in the Covid-19 cycle as a public health measure to reduce airflow between compartments. As an advanced paramedic on the joint Air Corps / NAS Emergency Aerom-

edical Service, Irelands premier HEMS operators, he had been taken aback one day when his military colleagues pointed out one day that while he was correct that they were useless for anti viral measures, thats not what they were for. What they really were, was a blast curtain designed to take some of the impact out of an explosion inside the Luas itself.

As the doors closed and the tram started to move, he missed the dull whump that echoed across the city. He hadn't looked at the news all day but was beginning to see that the tram was more crowded than normal and there was a tangible anxiety on his fellow commuters faces, masks or not. He looked again at his phone, scrolling through his messages. If he didn't already have a cold sweat going, this would've done the trick. He tasted coffee and jagermeister rising in the back of his throat and swallowed hard.

Reading down without opening each one he got enough of the story. 'Bombings, multiple, M50, all hands call in.' Bombing Dublin Airport, all hands call in' Bombing, Dublin Belfast train line, all hands call in' Bombing Heuston station, all hands... Those were the messages for the generic Whatsapp group. The last message directed to him was a straight forward 'Shane, answer your fucking phone and get to Baldonnel, they're standing up another heli for HEMS'.

On his feet now, his mind reeled through a plan, ok – get to the Red Cow, grab his car? No the roads will be jammed. Get a lift from the Gardai? There'll be none spare. Transport from Bal? Maybe, he could ring ahead for that. His phone rang again – Jerry. 'I got the messages just now, I'm on the Luas to get out there as quick as I can.'. The massive overpressure of an explosion (he never remembered an actual sound) prevented him hearing any response. Slammed to the ground along with everyone else, he got to his feet. The window beside him was shattered, spider webbed where it had been not quite blown out by the blast. The rubber curtains had blown inwards, knocking the women next to it into a seat occupied by an older man. He looked over, no apparent penetrating injuries. 'Looks like the curtains worked

122

after all' he thought before spotting what looked like a long nail stick-ing through the rubber mat at eye level. Quickly he realised that he could hear no screams from the other side of the cabin, only around him. He hoped that was just his hearing from the blast.

Pushing through the rubber mats, a few things occured to him all at once. He had thought from the force of it, that the blast originated in the next carriage. The first thing he could see, was that this was wrong, it was at least one carriage further down. This was apparent because that end of the carriage was missing, and a mix of blast and trauma injuries presented themselves in front of him. One younger man, early thirties maybe, stood standing at the end nearest to him looking at the dead and dying around him. Blood poured from his nose and ears and a white froth was growing at his mouth with each sucking breath. Further on he could see a woman, unmoving on the floor, her beige coat stained thoroughly red and a buggy on it's side that he already didn't want to approach.

The second thing that occured to him was 'Triage'. He had to priori-tise who to treat, who could be treated, before attending to anyone. Isn't that what they were thought on the Major Incident Medical Management course? Get organised or more will die than the one you're working on. The man in front of him slumped first to his knees and then bounced off a seat and onto the floor.

The last thing that occured to him as he looked down at his shaking hands, pulling on a pair of blue gloves and holding the small plastic face shield that he had pulled out of his bag at some point was that he didn't have enough of his kit with him to make any kind of differ-ence. Not nearly enough.

"Brendan" Red Team Member

'The Transport Bombings? Oh, there was a lot to unpack there wasn't there and from so many angles?To answer the first set of questions that always come up, yes; the plan was one of ours, almost a carbon copy of a risk assessment we had submitted over a year earlier. That's why the blast curtains had been fitted but that was about the only recomendation that was taken up. The second question that gets asked, no – of course we didn't fucking do it! At some point along the line, and it's still uncertain where, our information was compromised. You can't expect to go for this long in a war without someone on the other side having a success. Of proof, we have none, but all bets are that the securing of the risk assesment – basically that one was, how do you cripple Dublin in a day with maximum political and public effect? Well everyone knows that it that happened in a certain embassy in South Dublin who were probably a bit pissed off that they'd recently suffered some casualties.

Because that's what this was, right? Everyone wondered why the Carsonites laid off on the rocket attacks across the border, it's not like they decided to turn over a new leaf and turn to religion was it? No, as has been suspected from time to time, well somone took them out and I'm not saying outright it was us, but you know... What I said before, about work group targeting not being effective on the IRA, that was right, but that was for them. The same was largely true for the Carsonites, but the rocket teams were different. They needed more training, more supervision to be effective. That meant advisors from Russia on the ground.

We, well there's a whole other story in this but the Red Team is actually organised on the bones of a reactivated, old, FCA Battalion, the 16th Infantry. You have A Coy which does the opposition forces stuff for the staff course, all the low end stuff like that. B Coy, they do the risk assesments, all the looking around at our own country and asking themselves 'How would I kill that?' Then D Coy, who work in the cyberwarfare end of things, hacking, *kompromat* that kind of thing. Now, I'm not saying that there is a C Coy, but if there is, maybe they'd be the operational arm of the Red Team. The deniable ones doing things other people can't, right? If they exist at all...

So anyway, 'someone' targetted the rocket teams in their entirety. That included the advisors. That was deliberate, a bit of a definite fuck you right back kind of thing. And it worked, we didn't get all of them, but it stopped launches into Ireland. But Russia plays this game well, don't they?

The scheme of the transport bombings was to funnel people into a killzone unknown to themselves, while making the political and military forces look like they'd failed. It had a few stages. Step one, shut down the M50, the big ring road going all around Dublin. This was easy enough. One or two small, real, bombs go off without warning. This gives you the traffic jam. After that, you call in a mix of real and fake warnings for every bridge and junction along the way – they then all have to be treated as real.

You let that develop, get the EOD and Gardai out to deal with that, which is a shit show all on its' own, right? Then you hit the trains. Doesn't have to be an actual train itself, it's pretty easy to disrupt a train line, but they got best bang for their buck by doing it near Heuston and Connolly Stations. That way they cut both the East West and North South lines right there.

Then you top it off with hitting the ports in Dun Laoghaire and the airport itself – that was just a hacked drone dropping screws on the runways. Now, this is the genius bit, the really awful bit. Think of where people consume most of their media now, think of the graphics typically used by traditional and online news outlets when they have a bomb go off but can't get people to the scene for a photo? Look at all this on a screen the size of your typical smartphone.

Almost universally, there was a largescale map of Dublin with what was basically an explosion emoji over each of the modes of tranpost affected. A ring of them around the M50, no way out by air, by land or by sea. It looked for all the world - because almost no one zoomed in enough to see that there was still plenty of ways out, you could walk for a start- it looked like the city was being hemmed in and put under seige. No way out - except for the Luas. So the trams were crowded. This made it easier to get bombs on board and harder to spot them once they were there. That was the target all along, and the goal. Fifty two dead civilians on the trams themselves and another six out on the streets alongside them. All just normal people in the wrong place at the wrong time. And it had the planned effect didn't it? The government came under severe pressure, that came down on the security forces and when they found out it was one of our plans? We were almost disbanded and a big review then came on to 'regularise' our actions.

The Carsonites claimed it, why wouldn't they? If they could pull that off it would be a massive sign of their capability, and the media and politicians largely went with that. Proof is one thing, but I'd say the guys who planted those bombs strolled on back to their diplomatic immunity in South Dublin'

CHAP 7

Over reach

Most non state armed actors will, at some point, over reach beyond their inherent capabilities. Sometimes this is an over estimation of their abilities, sometimes it is a calculated risk in order to attain a political goal, sometimes it is a move of desperation to try to force a solution to their fight. This over reach usually takes the form of fighting as a conventional force when they don't have all the logistics, operational structures and training to go with it. Classic examples can are DeValeras' push to attack Dublin Castle that left seventy dead and captured, the outright expenditure of the NLF, or Viet Cong, by the North Vietnamese during the Tet offensive and more recently Isis presenting itself as a statelike construct and thereby making itself vulnerable to attacks on the supporting infrastructure of that pseudo state. It seems likely that the Carsonite push into Donegal in July 2022 will in the future be counted amongst the ranks of these strategic errors.

A quick summary of the military and political disposition of the key units involved is perhaps necessary at this point as the picture had already changed rapidly in the weeks preceeding the attacks and counterattacks described below.

During May, the fighting between Dissident and Carsonite groups escalalated sharply. This escalation occured on the back of a vague and wavering indication from Westminister that a second Scottish independence referendum might be held in a hazy but not to distant future after all. Far from sating the appetites of Scottish nationalists, they seized on this to make direct appeals to the UN to recognise Scottish independence as soon as it arose. Similar appeals were made to the EU for a strong statement that would guarantee membership on the day of Scottish independence, should that be the outcome of the ballot.

Regardless of any further statements from Westminister, the international media regarded the outcome as a sure bet and began to treat Scottish nationalist interviewees as members of a distinct state and government. This was especially the case with the US media who needed to fill airtime now that the post election violence had largely subsided with the rounding up of the last militias. Ineivitably, calls for an Irish border poll on the same day rose in unison. The effect on the Carsonite forces was to cause a terrifying mix of panic, rage and determination. The leadership of the group saw one way out – to double down on the policy of 'demographic change' – forcing out of Northern Ireland those that would potentially vote for Irish unity, or abstain, or simply not vote unionist enough for their liking.

By following this policy to its conclusion, it was felt that not only would the nationalist population be reduced, the British Army would be forced to intervene and almost certainly be drawn into greater conflict with the Dissidents, at which stage the Carsonites would present themselves as a friendly force willing to assist. Targeting was simple,predominantly nationalist areas were attacked, anyone found with an Irish passport, or indeed a passport from any EU nation, was killed. That this included several prominent unionists seemed to matter little as a kind of combat fatigue inspired bloodlust had settled on the organisation.

The Dissident forces were already on the back foot and struggling to maintain coherence. In several instances, they responded to Carsonite attacks and were promptly defeated by weight of numbers. With their strength now critically reduced below that necessary to compete with the Carsonites on the field, they simply adopted the tactics of their enemies and began attacking civilian populations centres where they could provoke a similar response – to drive people from their homes. On both sides of the divide, the effects of these campaigns of ethnic cleansing were exacerbated by online campaigns directed against the population – very simply, if one town was to be attacked, perhaps three would be singled out in online videos, tweets and other social media. The result was that one town would be put to the sword by violence and two more would see large amounts of houses and shops burned easily when the people living there had already fled for their lives.

This description sounds like a process that occured in distinct stages. In practice, the lines between phases and accountability for who moved first was blurred. A state of chaos became established and the PSNI, their temporary colleagues from the UK and small number of BA troops in Northern Ireland found themselves dealing with a humanitarian crisis. With a significant amount of people now made homeless and unable to return to their home towns, the security forces were compelled to establish IDP, or Internally Displaced People, camps in several rural areas which could more easily be controlled by the limited number of troops and police that could be spared from guarding vital installations such as power plants, water treatment plants and political and culturally important sites. All of these were being put to the torch as soon as they were left without security.

The population of Northern Ireland was now calling out for help and where it came from mattered little. Streams of refugees crossed the border and Ireland too found itself providing shelter for those who desperately needed it. Having, for once, a greater strategic depth – the area of the country away from the direct fighting - meant that Ireland was better able to disperse these refugees safely and without locally overwhelming any one area.

To the north however, the situation went from bad to worse in July when almost all the IDP camps were hit by large-scale coronavirus outbreaks. The distribution of vaccines in Northern Ireland had been severely hampered by the fighting and like most countries, had initially been targetted at the most high risk groups along with frontline professionals in the healthservices. Supply had become piecemeal at best when the pogroms started and herd immunity did not yet exist. The over-crowded camps became horrible petri dishes that favoured the disease. Calls for an international intervention increased from all corners and even in Westminister, the opposition benches favoured help from the outside, inside or anywhere. The be-leagured government, dealing with their own vaccine distribu-tion, the Scottish problem and trying to come to grips with the spiralling violence simply hardened their line. There would be no foreign intervention in UK domestic affairs.

In Ireland, the mood was one of 'the neighbours house is on fire, how do we help?' but also 'how do we stop this spreading?' Troops, Gardai and medical professionals were diverted to the humanitarian crisis with personnel from other EU countries also contributing field hospitals, to make up for a lack in the number of available Irish ones. Quietly, EU regular troops began to provide security for these hospitals in order to free up their Irish counterparts for other duties.

For all the build up of Irelands Defence Forces, there were still critical weaknesses. Most of the fighting had taken place in the eastern half of the border region. The vast expanses of border, both land and sea, in Donegal were heavily patrolled and ob-served by land, sea and air but to cover the whole inland border and coast with barracks and troops would have required an expansion many times that possible, just for that one county.

The end effect of this was that the main force protecting almost all of Donegal was the 28th Battalion based in Finner. This base had grown since earlier days and was now surrounded by permanent Observation Posts in a constellation around it. Some of these were more properly called hardpoints and included artillery and Javelin missile implacements as appropriate to their location. North of this, on the main road to Letterkenny, was Starfort 36, the last Starfort built and the last one still occupied, pending replacement by an under construction hardened barracks. One platoon strength detachment provided ATCP support to the Gardai in Letterkenny, another platoon plus sized detachment protected the major fishing port in Killybegs. A platoon of 2nd line reservists secured the airport on the North west coast, one of the very few areas where they formed a unit that large.

With so many gaps immediately apparent, given that the county was considered the gateway through which many of the seaborne weapons shipments in particular entered the country, patrolling was the order of the day. This required all of the 28Bn that could be spared from guarding fixed installations and reservists from many parts of the country, the population density of much of Donegal being too low to provide sufficient troops for its' size.

Helicopter led airmobile operations were routine, with the air picture in the country having improved markedly. The AW139 fleet had swollen to twelve airframes, the EC135 fleet had grown to eight and the more recent arrival of the first of an eventual five Chinooks in March were beginning to show dividends. The problem, as ever, was pilot, technician and aircrew numbers. The Air Corps was better equipped than ever, but the heli crews of No 3 Ops Wing were stretched and tired, having absorbed as much of the war as their compatriots on the ground. On the upside, the first six of eighteen Gripen fighters had landed in Baldonnel in early June. The extra airframes over and above the original twelve ordered had been requested as it became obvious that ground attack would indeed be a required role after all. For now, they were trained and equipped for air policing. The squadron commander, Comdt Mulvey, had already performed the first Irish Air Corps interception of a Russian aircraft within two weeks of arrival when flying as wingman for a French Rafale. Experience was being gained, but the numbers weren't there yet to stand up a twenty four hour QRA on their own.

Seperately, the Royal Navy carrier Queen Elizabeth continued it's undisclosed operations off the south west coast. It was normal, not to broadcast what they were doing, but under the circumstances people were more aware of the ships presence than might otherwise be the case.

But offshore and out of sight of land from the furthest west point of Kerry was along way from Donegal. It was in Ireland's most northern county that the Carsonites, reduced in number and also tired from continuous fighting, decided to force the issue and seek to bring the war to a close on their terms. On the night of the first of July 2022, the Carsonite forces invaded the Republic of Ireland.

Senator Ian Davis

'Militarily, we talk about key terrain. If you look at where Finner is, not far into the bottom of Donegal, the key terrain is to the North. First you come to the Bluestack Mountains, this chain starts in the East in Northern Ireland and runs West all the way to the coast. It is the dominant high ground splitting southern Donegal from the northern expanse of the county and Letterkenny town, the biggest population centre which was positioned about half way up. Letterkenny is itself at the bottom of Lough Swilly, a deep water fjord and also important coastal territory – much of the weapons that came in crossed Lough Swilly into the North, not including of course rumoured submarine activity.

The vital areas here were Letterkenny town as the biggest population centre, Killybegs as a major economic engine for the county and also a militarily important port in it's own right and the airport. All of these were north of the Bluestack Mountains and specifically, north of the Barnesmore Gap. This gap, which was in sight of Finner on a good day, was the gateway for the North of the county. Hold the gap and you hold the north. It consisted of a comparatively narrow, steep sided pass in the mountains with a river, a road and some phone lines at the base. Even the heli pilots treated it as a choke point, on the grounds that having to go around it by the coast, you might run out of fuel before you got back inland to your destination.

Of course, we weren't idiots, we knew this. In a previous life, I myself served in the Coy strength detachments in Rockhill, near Letterkenny and Fort Dun Ri, further north again but these were gone now, along with all the other outposts that disappeared in the 2012 reorg. They had been replaced as much as we could with Starfort 36 which sat just to the north of Barnesmore Gap itself, and the ATCP platoon in Letterkenny for Garda support along with the Reserve platoon in the airport and the regular platoon in Killybegs. In terms of fixed installations, that was it. It was always a case that counter insurgency operations in Donegal would have a focus on patrolling. The numbers required to permanently base enough troops all around the county and monitor every bit of activity from fixed positions would have used up the whole army. Instead, extensive use of helicopter borne airmobile patrolling was employed along with normal ground based patrolling and checkpoints.

The fact of the matter is, Donegal had been comparatively quiet, when you compare it to other areas of the border where the fighting was heaviest. It may be that the Dissidents didn't want to increase the heat in the area, when it was so vital to their resupply efforts – heavier combat would certainly have brought more attention to them there. It wasn't that we weren't doing everything we could to interdict wepons already, it's that we were still stretched thin. If the fighting was in the East and you have a finite amount of people and equipment, that's where it had to go.

Donegal became a place where, so much as we could, we sent new Lts, new Ptes there first to cut there teeth before throwing them into the fight. It wasn't always possible but it was observable that those personnel had a lower attrition rate than ones who had their first detachment in Starfort 4 or the Sliabh Blooms for example. In short, apart from Finner in the South of the county, Donegal was low on numbers and experience for the size of the county. Troops mounted their patrols by helicopter into the northern parts of the county, with the occasional amphibious landing around the coast with the Naval Service just to keep everyone guessing. It was often littered as well with recce troops and ARW on longer term patrols monitoring suspected supply lines, but these were often intelligence lead operations – if the enemy air activity picked up, we knew arms were coming in one way or another and we would deploy them then, otherwise high end experienced troops were needed elsewhere.

Many questions have been asked as to why we didn't do X,Y or Z to put more troops into Donegal. People putting these suggestions forward typically have no idea how long it actually takes to reinforce and rebuild an Army once it has been run down in numbers – it's more than just rushing people through six months of recruit training. The experience of the leadership on the ground is critical, the NCOs and junior officers. Even with years of combat now under our belt, and the re-entrants with overseas experience, the more we grew, the thinner the experience was spread. It was a direct consequence of the accelerated process we were forced to employ, a risk we knowingly took. We certainly reaped the consequences. It must also be remembered, that no one was expecting an attack like this, not even the Russians. Even the Carsonites didn't expect it to work out like it eventually did. What they envisaged as a large scale raid, turned into multiple smaller actions of their own and then into a rout.

That complete surprise that they achieved on the first day and their actions, as viewed by us on the outside of their command element, meant that in the ensuing political panic, notions were entertained about British intentions that even now at this short remove seem outlandish, but which at the time were plausible. That the British government were also taken by surprise and were... uncommunicative, did not help. Moving their carrier further North instead of clearing the combat area; almost certainly it was what they said it was, merely an attempt to keep an eye on events but it looked like an aggresive move.

It was seen as unlikely, but what if the mood towards the Carsonites had changed and now they had air support from carrier launched stealth fighter? The one percent chance possibility meant it couldn't be ruled out which lead to the next question. What would the French do? They had signed on for a peacetime air policing effort, not a confrontation with F 35s from a NATO state with all the Article 5 implications that might have. Would they still police the air environment under those circumstances? Which lead straight to the follow up – our own fighter fleet was brand new and not yet equipped for air to ground operations, would the French assist in that arena, one that was clearly outside the original agreement. This took tense negotiation over several crucial days.

Add to this the fear of further bombings in Dublin and else-where, and the increasingly acrimonious tension within the British Govt itself regarding both the war in the North and the Scottish independence movement, all of which was being played out in the media. Yes, the mood was certainly tense. Fearful. Febrile. Wrong moves either at the tactical level or the political level, in any of the relevant capitol cities, could have lead us all to a violent place we didn't want, or intend to be.'

The Carsonite attack into Donegal opened up with a heavy rocket barrage onto Starfort 36. The platoon there, the fort was understrength compared to its design, were overwhelmed by a mix of hi explosive and thermobaric warheads. Any that survived the first, were killed by either the blast, heat or suffica-tion effects of the latter. This effectively opened the door into northern Donegal and the left out patrol was quickly snapped up by the mobile forces that followed on the heels of the last rocket. Estimates vary, but most say that as many as five hun-dred Carsonite fighters, riding on four wheel drive vehicles that were themselves equipped with machine gun, rocket and mor-tar support weapons, entered the area North of the Barnesmore Gap and began to spread out.

Most formed a defensive base in the windfarm known as the Donegal Cluster. The apparent intention was that the undu-lating, rocky hills, along with the windmills and anemometer masts, would deter a direct helicopter assualt on their forces. The tracks running through the area to give access to mainten-ance vehicles for the windfarm allowed them to swiftly move the location of their support weapons and to mass quickly to see of any assault. These tracks and their access points were, of course, dialled in for defensive fire from their mortars and machine guns, along with the entries to the hills being laced with IEDS. These positions were further covered by a company strength detachment who occupied the high points of the Blue-stack Mountains themselves, with machine gun, mortar and as, it was unfortunately discovered, surface to air missiles. Hi-jacked vehicles were used to block the road at it's narrowest point. These were also quickly fitted with IEDs and covered by machine gun fire from emplacements further up the steep sided hills. The Barnesmore Gap was now closed.

Subsequent debriefing of captured Carsonite fighters revealed that even at this point, the intention they had been briefed on was ambitious. They were to establish temporary dominance in the area, seek out and destroy any Irish forces they could take on in greater numbers, destroy such infrastructure as they could find to include police stations, post offices and any other target that would impair the normal running of society and to 'improve the demographic situation'. This last goal was gener-ally seen as an order to kill or otherwise drive from the area any civilians they could find. Then, after several days to a week of raiding, they would withdraw across the border having dem-onstrated they were a force to be reckoned with, thereby force-fully ensuring the union between Northern Ireland and Britain. Regretfully, it went well at first, although the counter attack was coming.

D-1

Comdt Dave Heally

'Contrary to what alot of people wanted to do, Christ, some of the comments on Twitter were ridiculous, you have to plan these things if you want them to work. You can't just charge in half cocked and expect that it will go well. Yes, it took days to get moving. Yes, people died as a result. No, it couldn't have been done quicker. Remember it wasn't clear cut at that stage, we had to gather intelligence the hard way – that fighting patrol from 28 Bn that got chewed up approaching the Gap, that Air Corps Spectre that just about made it to Sligo airport with half it's wing missing? Unfortunately, sometimes, that's how you find things out about your enemy's strength.

I was still in touch with Capt Brian Quinlan at that point, he was in Ops in DFHQ and he told me the mood there was 'busy but calm'. That surprised me, given the chaos eleswhere, but he said that some of the big decisions were made early enough and then it was just flat out doing the staff work and planning. Remember, there were raids going on all this time north of Barnesmore, there was that carrier off the coast, all along the border, no one knew what would happen next. 'Busy but calm'. Fair enough if they were, I'll give them that.

According to Brian, the first things that came up was the platoons in Letterkenny and Killybegs. They were told to just melt away and send back intelligence. What else could they do? Patrol the town, be seen to be seen and then get destroyed by weight of numbers? No, they were more useful doing it they way they did. The reserve platoon in the airport was different, they reckoned they could hold out a bit, just because of their location, it was further removed from the intial breakthrough, wasn't on any of the main roads, they had more time. They rigged the whole airport for destruction anyway, just in case.

The main meat of the counterattack was going to be 2 Cav. They had swollen from being a armoured car squadron to being the national QRF, the same size as an infantry battalion but with more armoured vehicles. They were based in the Curragh though and it was pretty clear that on their own, they wouldn't be enough. That's where we were to come in.

We were still technically part of 1 Bn North East on the books, we had been relieved on the border, but we were still in the Curragh doing all the wind down stuff, PSS debriefings, Lessons Learned all that stuff. The result being, when they needed another battalion at short notice that had all their annual weapons training, heli drills, dismount drills, all that stuff up to date? Well, we were sitting right there. No brainer from a staff point of view, I know, but it was a hard pill to swallow. Then again, everyone was going to want a piece of the fight eventually, just these troops were tired. They'd already mentally checked out back into the reorg and resupply mode between border tours. It took as long as the first messages back from Finner to get through for people to get motivated again. Games were over at that point weren't they?

So, overall. The plan was that 2 Cav, plus a few other armoured sub units they picked up along the way in the Curragh, would open and hold the road between the Barnesmore Gap and Letterkenny, preventing any reinforcements entering the area from the East. We were to be driven up to Finner, where we would meet up with the Air Corps helis and assault onto the top of the Bluestacks. 28 Bn would then drive through in the soft skin transport we arrived in, around the same time, to surround, dismount and engage the enemy in the Donegal Cluster. Artillery was being brought up that would engage the Bluestack targets, but the only strike and close air support we were to have was PC-9s – they were still sorting things out with the French at that point. The area would then be back filled with reservists who were being dragged up from, well, wherever we could find any. Plenty of holes in that plan at first glance, isn't there? Well we found a few more didn't we. Nevertheless, the situation had gone about as far as it could be allowed to and had to be stopped. We got a nice new name and were sent on our way.'

D Day

Comdt Brian Rafferty AC Ret'd

'This was to be the first big day out for the Chinooks, we could only spare two to the operation, three for the first day, but two afterwards because we were stripping out every other aircraft we could afford to from the border. You're always going to have some on maintenance so for that first lift in, we had three Chinooks at fifty five troops a piece, wedged in, and six AW139s at nine a piece. We had four EC135s as well for recce and sniping in theory, but in practice, two of them were calling in the PC-9s more than anything else. So yeah, not in bad shape really, we were going to be able to put nearly all of Task Group Viking, as they were now called since there was an actual 1 Bn North East on the border, we'd get nearly them all in place in two lifts from Finner for that first assault.

The weather was holding, but a weather forecast in Donegal is really a 'what have you done for me lately kind of thing'. Hurt us bad after a few days. Anyway, we got to Finner and the place was barely organised chaos. The runway was packed, the refuellers that came up with the convoy were nearly empty with all the aircraft that were there. There was troops bivvying up in the dunes – we saw them on the way in and thought they were security but they just had no where else to go, the place was wedged and 2 Cav hadn't even arrived yet, the softskin convoy had left before them and gotten the troops up first. Thank God there was no one with a mortar dialled in on the place because it would've been carnage.

We actually ended up doing two extra resupply runs with the Chinooks, just to bring up fuel and hot meals, the place was overwhelmed because obviously notice was short, no one had time to order extra rations a month out, did they?

Anyway, that first assault. It was the next day, so the third day after the initial Carsonite attack. 2 Cav had rolled out in the morning, we had asked to go for a night assault, but the PC9s and the ground troops still didn't have enough night vision to go around. It all had a bit of a 'walking towards the machine guns vibe', going in by day. The worry was that there would be a push south of the gap into Donegal town and at that stage, it would not be self contained to the North and would spread south. Anyway, daytime it was.

The running order for us was the two EC135s running forward air control for the PC-9s, two AW139s with troops to secure landing sites for the Chinooks on the Western end of the Bluestacks, two Chinooks following close behind them and then us with the other four AW139s and last Chinook on our Eastern side. We were all split up into flights but the need to put sufficient troops in place meant we were all essentially in two big tactically spaced out trains. Because we were assaulting mountain tops, we were also already up at altitude, which sucked. It's worth pointing out that, yes, we'd been assaulting through the Cooleys and all that, but running straight at a hot LZ with a SAM threat? One that had already hit one of the Spectres? This was fairly new to all of us, so yeah, it's fair to say there was a lot of nerves before take off. Once we got up and going though, there was too much going on to do anything except, well, just do it, get on with it. It wasn't going to get any better for waiting at that stage!

Obviously, we had prepped the area, such arty as was available had hit our LZ just before we got there but a few miles out still. We split off East and the rest split off west. After trying to avoid the back end of a Chinook, the first big picture I saw when he cleared out of my way had quite a bit to take in. First, on the ground on the east, on my side. I saw the last few rounds splash on top of the mountains, where we were going to land. I saw smoke coming out of the Barnesmore Gap itself, where 2 Cav had only just pushed through, just then. There were two Mowags burning on the side of the road just south of it where they'd been pushed out of the way and the others were just steaming through, having blown up the roadblocks and you could still see where everyone was engaging the machine gun nests on the hills as they rolled through, no stopping.

The one that had my eyes popping though was the little thin threads of smoke, missiles, streaking up off the mountains on the West. The PC-9s were meant to hit that LZ with rockets and machine guns. I don't know if any section of them had rolled in before that, but just after the missiles went up, a barrage of rockets came right back down on top of them. I was craning my head around to see what happened to the missiles, but once I looked up, I could see a PC-9, burning. Wherever the missile had actually hit them, the whole left wing was ablaze with big orange streaks behind them, the fuel was going up, you know? Once they were turned out to sea, they punched out. I didn't see that happen, but one of the other AW139s went out to pick them up after the second troop drop.

We were only seconds out at this stage, and the rest was actually pretty routine. I didn't get shot at on that drop, I know a few of the other helis did alright and the Chinooks were real bullet magnets, but we just came into a hover on the right of the formation, everyone else out to the left of us, doors were already open at that point and the troops were nearly gone before I gave the 'clear deploy'. I think they knew as well as we did it was a fairly high risk approach for a heli to take into an area. We did a spot turn to the east at that stage, nice and light and just dove away down the hill downwind. The gunner on the left side called a target and my copilot gave him the clear engage, they both had eyes on it, but I actually saw none of the enemy up close on the first go.'

◆ ◆ ◆

The fighting on that first day had mixed results. 2 Cav cleared the road allowing access up as far as Letterkenny, where the ATCP platoon were probably the happiest people in the town to see them. They then concentrated on keeping the road secure – a big ask for one battalion. The airmobile assault on the Bluestacks cost three lives and eleven injured but was succesful in the capturing almost all of the Carsonite fighters who realised that they're was no way off the mountain for them. Others chose to fight to the death and were obliged, with airstrikes and artillery continuing throughout the day. There was also the loss of a PC-9 to a surface to air missile and one of the EC135s was badly damaged by machine gun fire late in the afternoon. One fixed wing pilot suffered back injuries on ejecting from his burning aircraft, but the heli crew got away unharmed.

The biggest problem of the day however was that, despite hard fighting up the side of the hills, 28 Bn had not been able to dislodge the enemy from the windfarm at the Donegal Cluster. Suffering seventeen wounded, they had been forced to withdraw from the engagement and, along with the Task Group Viking, began to adopt blocking positions around the area. Overnight, an attempted breakout to the east was stopped by the combined efforts of 2 Cav, 28 Bn and TG Viking. While this enegagement was still going on however, approximately one hundred and fifty Carsonite fighters in their vehicles, pushed through the reduced perimeter on the western side and escaped. To make a bad night worse, the weather which had been acceptable so far began to close in. Day two of the fight would be fought in unexpectedly bad conditions, while the fighters that escaped the western perimeter broke into small groups and disappeared.

D+1

Cpl Diane Keane

'The weather turned worse overnight, I don't think anyone slept, regardless of whether they were on or off sentry duty. The visibility was terrible, we could hear the fighting going on over on the east side, but you could only see the occasional flash to go with it. Our side on the west, we knew they were getting out in small numbers. It was so frustrating. We had one contact, two jeeps on one of the tracks. We had cleared a roadblock on the first day and advanced passed it and set up an ambush there. We were still overlooked by the hills on our left, so I had two of mine up there for flank security. Couldn't see them even that little bit away, so it was going to be radio comms with them. We heard the vehicles coming down the hill before we saw them. They were just freewheeling down, no engine noise but you could hear the gravel and tyre noise crunching on the track. They came around a bend to our front, we let them get close enough to even the odds, the front vehicle had what looked like a .50 machine gun on the back. We had just our own personal weapons, nothing like a claymore or anything like that even, so when they got close enough, maybe twenty metres we just opened up on the silhouettes. Once we fired, they put on their headlights and just floored it. The machine gunner was just shooting straight down the track, I don't think he ever even saw us. That first vehicle got through, and just kept going. The second one, a 40mm grenade hit it in the grill and went off, stopping it dead. We just kept piling in the rounds until there was clearly nothing left to fight. We found four dead there and a mortar lying flat in the back of it. Tough night, but nothing else came down that way.

Next morning, the weather hadn't cleared. Instead of seeing

nothing but black, it was nothing but grey. I don't think anyone tried to break out that day. There was one or two attempts to push in with platoon size patrols but people were just stepping on top of Carsonite machine gun pits and IEDs. They cut that out after lunchtime and kept pressure on by lobbing in a few mortars now and again, but we stood fast all that day. It was still reckoned there was about two hundred plus support weapons equipped fighters alive in there so you didn't just wander right in. I know our Coy HQ tried sending in a drone to have a look but it just flew off and crashed.'

The cause of the drone crash that frustrated Cpl Keane was actually part of a bigger problem. GPS jammers had been brought in by the Carsonites for exactly that reason. Most drones know where they are in space and are told where to go by using GPS rather than actually being directly flown. With this being locally jammed they simply would not get off the ground. When this safety feature was over ridden , they crashed. This caused problems for the Air Corps too, who were experiencing degraded navigational performance even up to several thousand feet up. This meant parachute drops of supplies were out of the question as they could just as easily resupply the enemy. Helicopters were already unable to push through the bad weather such was the lack of visibility even without their navigation systems being affected close to the target. Although, using their radars, they had spent the entire day dropping down over the water and bringing ammunition and reservists into Finner, from where they were bussed out each time enough had arrived to be able to properly secure a convoy.

Of great importance was the fact that close air support was not immediately possible. The French government had actually given permission for their QRA aircraft to fly close air support missions the previous evening, with the shooting down of the PC-9 undeniably proving the need. However, they had laid down clear rules of engagement – targets must be visually verified by the pilot. Under no circumstances did they want a friendly fire incident coming back on them. This would not generally have been a problem. The targetting pods being flown out for the Rafales, along with a supply of laser guided bombs, were absolutely capable of picking out targets by day or night. They would then use the pods own laser to designate the target for the bombs and *voila*. Except the pods, whether using daylight cameras or infra red ones, still needed to see the target which heavy cloud cover ruled out.

With the frantic ISR scramble going on to find the escaping Carsonites, the airspace was already busy and needed management anyway, but the end result was that air power could not be applied effectively until D+2.

D+2

Lt Eamonn 'Rover' Byrne

'I guess they just didn't know how much pilots hate windfarms. I mean, if they thought that they wouldn't get hit because that infrastructure was there? Any pilot is going to look at that, all those poxy half invisible masts and low level obstacles? You just look at that and think ' have I got a bigger bomb for this?'. That looks like the French frame of mind too. We were flying top cover, me and the boss, up at altitude providing a CAP, Combat Air Patrol. To be honest, I think we were just flying the flag a little at that point? Who were we capping against really? The French were doing the bombing. We all flew up from Shannon in close formation, not the norm but we were told the press office wanted pictures. I was Echelon Starboard to the boss, so sitting a bit back off his right wing and the Rafales were all to the right of me. When they tipped in to hit the target, the guy nearest me gave a thumbs up and rolled the plane over. I got the full view of the underside – fuel tanks, standard load of air to air Mica missiles and those big bombs. You hear 2000lb bomb and it sounds big, but when you see the size of them on the aircraft , they're huge things.

The brief we got was that the Army wanted to make a clean cut of things that morning, They lost a day with the weather and wanted the whole business in the Donegal cluster over with so they could chase down the breakout groups. So the Rafales loaded up their heaviest weapons and headed out. Each plane carried one impact fused and one air burst weapon. The idea was that not only would any targets be directly destroyed but the shockwaves would take out the IEDs as well. Four jets dropping four thousand pounds of bombs on a target that size is a lot of bang. I was at twenty thousand feet and it looked like the whole area just disappeared under a mushroom cloud, I'm nearly certain I heard it too.'

Comdt Dave Heally

'If they worked out what was happening, it didn't really matter. We pulled everyone back as far as they could go with the little notice we gave them. I've never seen anything like it before, or since. The explosion itself was huge, I think everyone kind of went 'oh fuck'. As soon as it was safe to move in, it takes time for debris to fall down again after that size of a blast, we stormed in hard and fast, just took our chances that there might still be IEDs functional. It was more or less unnecessary. There was practically no fighting, the sheer shock factor was enough and we policed up the survivors pretty quick. We took eighty four living prisoners off that hill, although I believe two of them died of their injuries in hospital. The scene was eerie you know?

Completely destroyed, the whole windfarm was gone.'

This third day of operations saw the first use of heavy airstrikes in Ireland since the Civil War. The swiftness with which they effectively drew a line under an operation that would otherwise have cost more Irish soldiers lives was not ignored in Dublin. As quickly as the bombs had brought that battle to a close, complaints flooded in. Concern from London was voiced about the use of such firepower against those who were, acts of war aside, still UK citizens. This concern was not directed towards Ireland however, but towards the French government and Brussels. The story was being pitched in the tabloid media as an extension of the EU / UK negotiations.

With a carrier now closing on the combat area, there was worry in Dublin that 'concern' could lead to 'conflict'. Mixed messages from different factions within the UK governement did not help issues. Was the official party line, that the carrier was only training and that there would be no intervention in Irish matters the correct one? How about the vague but belicose leaks to the press from hardliners that threatened airstrikes if the French did not stop bombing? And even then, airstrikes on who and where? It was all caught up and muddled in the headline driven fog of war. Clarity was lacking and as Rafales and Gripens were tasked to mount a standing CAP over Galway in order to cover both the Northwest and Shannon, the warm, sunny afternoon and evening of that summer day were tense.

If a Rafale or Gripen encountered an F35 off the west coast, what would happen. No one knew, rules of engagement were unclear apart from do not fire until fired upon (a fairly useless rule in air combat, albeit the only likely scenario if the Irish or French jets were engaged in earnest by the stealth fighters). Those hours were perhaps the closest to an accidental war the EU has come.

In the meantime, Irish Air Corps Spectre ISR airplanes along with EC135 and AW139 helicopters searched for Carsonite breakout forces. Some undoubtedly made it across the border. Most however, as many as a hundred by the final tally, continued in the same direction as their earlier breakout. West. They appeared to be making best speed towards the airport. As individual groups were spotted, they were cordoned off by airmobile troops and fixed in place, with the more heavily armed ground troops doing the destroying. In many cases however, the ground forces were out of position and a real threat to the airport began to emerge.

Comdt Dave Heally

'We had spent most of the day, moving troops from A to B by helicopter in order to try and get a fix on the enemy and just bring this thing to a stop. The troops were exhausted, some of them slept on the helis until they were needed to go back into the fight, again. By the evening, it was pretty clear that no matter what we came across, unless we had overwhelming numbers, it was time to just track the target and pull back a bit – you can only ask so much of people before they can give no more. Most of them had no sleep in days, I know I'd only grabbed bits here and there. Where possible, we called in airstrikes. I know there was a lot going on politically at that time, but the French were still there overhead, dropping smaller bombs this time and strafing with their cannons. They were still staying up over ten thousand feet though, leaving it for us to plug away down in the threat band for shoulder launched missiles. Can't blame them, I would too and they were still getting the job done.

Once night fell, we were called back to Finner and it was left to the ISR aircraft to track targets where they could, but it was still a case that we couldn't account for all of them – we still didn't know how many had gone across the border or if there was still a significant force out there heading for the airport and why? Were they expecting an extraction? By who?

Anyway, it made no difference for us. We thought we might get a rest but no, 28 Bn and 2 Cav were out of position to provide troops for air ops, they were busy moving west on the ground. So, lucky us, we got to move by heli again, this time around the coast and all the way up to the airport to reinforce the reserve platoon. They were apparently losing their minds listening to everything that was happening by way of piecemeal briefings coming their way. They were apparently given a 'be prepared to' order to blow up the facilities there, which was then rescinded and then reordered again. So it was back on the Chinooks.

Their crews looked dead on their feet as well, they'd been flying in reservists from wherever they could get them since the start of the operation. The AW139s were apparently flown out and needed to be serviced. Something to do with having all of them operational at once ruining a maintenance plan, according to one of their pilots. I couldn't relly follow what he was talking about to be honest, we were both wrecked. We were assured we'd have two back in the morning. Two, like, out of a whole fleet.There was one still on medevac standby in Finner, along with two EC135s that were doing mostly local patrolling by then.

So, we landed in the airport in a couple of runs, the first one brought all of what we had left of TG Viking, at this point down to two full Coys plus one and a bit platoons. The second wave brought in a company of reservists. The guys at the airport were well on edge by that point and I'm nearly surprised we weren't fired on when we approached, they'd been hanging out on their own there for the week and were starting to jump at shadows. The new reserve guys that we brought in, well lets just say they took a bit of organising. I don't want to seem like I'm going to town on them, it's just... this was the first time that I personally saw where the chunks had been cut out of their training, I'll put it that way. These guys who were absolutely top of their game in small unit patrolling, four person squads, you know, up to a section of nine. But put them into a bigger formation and they weren't used to it, didn't always know what to do or where to be. They hadn't been trained for it and, really this was not the time to have to learn. It was a long night getting set up, but we got there.'

As the night of D + 2 drew on, a firmer grasp of the situation was coming into view. The Carsonites remaining, judged now to be between eighty and one hundred, had managed to escape and evade in small groups as far west as a place called Mullaghderg Mountain, a rocky outcrop between the N56 and R259 roads and only three and a half kilometres from Donegal Airport in a straight line. It was as far as they would go. Two more airstrikes during the night had fixed them in place, giving time for the weary troops of 28 Bn and 2 Cav to make their way into position around them to the South and West, with TG Viking and the reserve units to their north east. As day broke, they had nowhere to go.

D + 3

All morning, calls for surrender were being met with rifle fire, with the heavy weapons seemingly having been abandoned or out of ammunition. The position of the Carsonites at this time was clearly untenable, but they were nevertheless still a force that could pose lethal risk. The area was one that could be costly for a straightforward infantry attack. At all levels, the country had it's fill of costly battles. Necessity was one thing, but this battle was one that the enemy was choosing for their own reasons, maybe to go down fighting, maybe to just take as many with them as possible. It was decided at DFHQ, not, in this case to oblige.

Lt Eamonn 'Rover' Byrne

'Costa was not happy when she heard, she'd been on CAP most of the night, otherwise it would've been her. We'd swapped shifts because she needed the night flying currency, you need to fly a certain amount a month in different flight regimes and she needed some night work. But that's how it goes. It was actually one of the French guys who came up with the idea, not specifically for this mission but in general to get us bombing. The pressure was coming on from on high to get us in the fight supporting the land component, obviously we didn't have the training done for it so we had to come up with something.

What he came up with was that we'd basically be the bomb truck, hauling weapons for someone else. We'd tuck in on the wing of a Rafale with two, five hundred pound, laser guided bombs. The Rafale would use it's pod to designate the target and we'd drop when he gave the word. As he said, 'the bomb doesn't care where its dropped from as long as it sees the laser.' Apparently it worked well enough for them in the Sahel with Mirage jets, that's where he'd seen it before. So, this became the plan. Myself and the boss were flying around, each paired up with a Rafale, waiting for the call. The bosses flight was just hooking up on the tanker, like, literally the exact moment when they couldn't come back in when the task came through to us in the afternoon. We were already practically overhead, we'd made a point of making noise over them all day, so we actually had to extend back out to the west to make our run.

Apparently, they had decided in HQ that this was it, no more offers of surrender just to get shot at in return. This wasn't exactly a warning shot, apparently the direction was 'pick a small group and take them out' or words to that effect. 28 Bn supplied the coordinates, which were duly dialled up by the pilot of the Rafale. We tipped in high from about twenty thousand, shallow dive angle. I'll be honest, I was just working hard on staying as close in formation as I could and not messing that up. I actually missed the reticule appearing on my head up display in front of me saying 'there's a target being designated for you'. I just held the formation and when the lead said release, I released.

He levelled off and turned away to the south, still tracking the target. I broke off to the left and climbed. I'm not going to lie, I rolled passed ninety degrees angle of bank to look up through the canopy at the ground to see the impact. Big flash of brown dirt being thrown up, but I didn't make out much else, no huge explosion. I went back to just flying the plane at that stage and rejoined with the lead. The boss was off the tanker at that point and steaming back in, so it was pretty clear we wouldn't get another shot if it came up. We headed off to the tanker then for fuel when the bosses flight replaced us. I believe we'd just plugged in when the surrender came through. And that was it, the first Irish Air Corps airstrike of the new jet age and the most historic since Fitzmaurice shot up Fermoy.'

The bombing of the this one target was not unique, the French had already carried out several attacks as already described. What was different was that it was an Irish aircraft dropping the weapon. It was presented in the media as an Irish airstrike with suitable pictures of a bombed up Gripen departing Shannon, and a comparison shot of one returning with one wing lacking a weapon. The fact that this was not yet a mature capability that could be delivered without French assistance was glossed over to create the desired impression: the Air Corps could now carry out close air support without fear of shoulder launched surface to air missiles, using weapons far more accurate and effective than the unguided rockets launched from the vulnerable PC-9s.

Backing up this initial bluff, the pilots, technicians and armourers still training in Sweden had their courses extended to cover the full range of air to air, air to ground and anti shipping missions. This capability, once it existed would provide the ability to engage targets within Ireland without the political twisting and turning required to get a third party nation to do it. It also meant that a realistic and accurate counter to cross border rocket attacks now existed, should they reoccur. Firing a counter battery of artillery at an unseen target in Northern Ireland carried huge political risks in terms of hitting civilians or civilian housing and infrastruture. A jet firing a single missile from within Irish airspace at a target they could see and record with their targeting pod was an entirely different scenario. It would preclude the use of such attacks altogether or at very least push the launch sites so deep into Northern Ireland as to blunt their effectiveness.

The writing by now was very clearly on the wall for semi conventional cross border attacks into Ireland. A combination of combat losses and indigenous air power meant that they would simply not be an option that any non state organisation like the Carsonites or Dissidents could survive. Unfortunately, in the world of asymmetric warfare, there is always a way to achieve your aim. The darkest day for Irelands Defence Forces was just around the corner, and the consequences of forgetting that you had rushed training would be brought into stark relief.

CHAP 8

Operation Armageddon 2

This is hell. All Cpl Lukasz McGrath could come up with was 'This is hell'. It wasn't new. It wasn't original. But it pretty much summed it all up. Pinned down in dead ground with tracers flying over their heads, his section was spread out so that one burst of machine gun fire couldn't kill all of them. Looking across to his right, he could see Jan Nowaks section doing the same. Looking the other way, all he could see of the section on his left was two soldiers crawling towards his position. The remaining seven, lacking the slight dip in the ground that was giving his troops a bit of respite from the incoming fire, they'd just been chewed up completely. One of the crawling soldiers slid like a worm into the comparative safety beside Lukasz.. His comrade, about a metre behind him jerked once and lay still as a burst of rounds found his head and back. The new arrival looked at Lukasz with eyes wide with shock at the sudden reversal of fortune they had suffered. He wondered how useful the boy would be when they had to move, because they sure as hell couldn't stay here.

Daring to raise his head an inch off the ground to look over his shoulder, he could see the convoy still getting lit up with machine gun and RPG fire. One Mowag and several soft skin vehicles were burning. Others were just stopped, occasionally rocking as a rocket frgagment or bullet hit some part solid enough to sway the trucks back and forth. The ground around them was littered with dead and wounded, civilians and soldiers, who'd tried to escape the barrage of fire. Literally, there were piles of them at the back of each tailgate.

He had no idea where his platoon commander was, he'd seen the platoon sergeant go down in the first volley of fire, so it was a safe assumption the Lieutenant was dead too. His dip in the ground was the whole world now, though a fairly fragile one. His brain was somewhat getting over the shock of the ambush and starting to evaluate things. One mortar in here and all of them were done. After what had seemed like an eternity, he finally heard the turreted wepons on the remaining Mowags open up. It didn't seem to do much to quieten the incoming fire but, if they stayed here a bit longer, then maybe... He didn't know where it came from but up and down the line of soldiers he heard something even worse than the screams. 'Ar aghaidh' – 'Forward'. They were attacking into the ambush. What was left of his company was attacking into the ambush. Oh Fuck. This is hell.

An Sráid Gan Áthas

When the remains of the escaping Carsonite force withdrew into Northern Ireland, it was clear to them and to all other observers that the game had changed dramatically. In a matter of days, they had been transformed from being the dominant paramilitary force, one that had leveraged the split between the IRA and the Dissidents to devastating effect; and which had felt sure enough of itself to launch a large scale raid across the border; into something quite different. In terms of pure numbers, they were now more or less equal with the Dissidents. They had however expended a lot of materiel as well as personnel in attacking Donegal. How much? No one knew outside of themselves, but there was definitely blood in the water.

The Carsonite commanders were now obliged to assert themselves somewhere. Really, they had no option. To melt away in small groups was to invite attack by Dissidents, and piecemeal destruction. To fail to act was to allow the battered morale of their fighters to worsen, which again invited destruction of a different kind – demoralised troops are prime hunting ground for intelligence agencies seeking an 'in'. To quietly reorganise was to risk being cut off from resupply by Russia – a quiet terrorist is not a relavent one when political and media distraction is your goal and they could easily feed those arms to other more active groups. Again, this was to invite destruction.

So an attack was necessary – an aggressive action showing they were still to be feared and would not be picked off by the circling sharks. But who and where? It had to be an undeniable victory or it would just worsen their situation. The answer was only days in coming.

Located just twenty kilometres across the border and only thirty kilometres from Finner, was the IDP camp known as Camp Erne, named for Lough Erne which was just to the North. Positioned at a crossroads between the A46 and Binmore road, the camp had become a clearing ground for IDPs who wanted to cross into Ireland and the EU. Although it housed all comers , with a split close to fifty/fifty in terms of background, the fact that they were trying to get across the border made it a politically 'safe' target for the Carsonites, in their own minds at least. In the shocked state of their fighters however, operational security - the control of information relevant to an upcoming mission - had broken down just enough to allow intelligence agencies on both sides of the border to put together details of the attack from social media. The PSNI personnel guarding the camp insisted that they needed to be reinforced with troops or the camp had to be evacuated, that they could not successfully defend the people there against a full scale attack.

Here once more, the political situation muddied the response. Unknown to the EU, the USA was once more offering personnel to assist with security in Northern Ireland and specifically with the defence of IDP camps. This time backroom, unofficial, pressure was being applied to allow in Private Military Contractors, or mercenaries in plain language. These contractors had a long and storied past in the War on Terror , one that the UK had no intention of reinvigorating so close to home. Equally, a troop deployment so close to the border would be considered provacative, regardless of the genuine reasoning.

So it was that, with many conditions, the UK gave permission for an EU humanitarian force to evacaute Camp Erne into Ireland. This came as a surprise in Dublin, Brussels and Paris. There was little doubt that the Irish troops, being so close to the scene would be the ones to respond. However, under the existing Triple Lock, any foreign deployment of more than twelve Irish military personnel required approval from both the Dail and the Seanad, and the UN security council. Since the Good Friday Agreement had removed the constitutional claim on Northern Ireland, crossing twenty kilometres over the border counted as a foreign deployment. Even with a non-permanent seat on the Security Council, the diplomatic work to gain approval was as frenetic as the military planning. It was all impossible to keep out of the media. Both the Dissidents and the Carsonites adjusted their plans accordingly.

Comdt Dave Healy

' I mean, apart from the proximity and the timelines, it was the planning restrictions that put us in the crosshairs for this job again. The UK knew they were rowing back ,politically, so they couldn't let us go in too strong – as busy as we were, you couldn't miss the news coming out of Westminister. Humanitarian or not, this was not a popular decision to let us in. At the very least, it was being used as a stick to beat the government, at best there was a 'why aren't we doing this ourselves' mood. Either way, we were left with some bitter pills to swallow on our end.

The first was numbers. We could bring as many soft skin vehicles and drivers as we wanted but in terms of security – fighting troops – we were limited to a battalion. So that was anyone in a Mowag or the back of a heli. Air was the next thing – no fighters. I think the French were happy enough about that, bombing Carsonites attacking in Ireland is one thing, but bombing UK passport holders in Northern Ireland? Whole different political deal. Almost as bad was that we could only use our own helicopters to insert and extract. No recce machines and no reinforcing or manouvering units if we got into trouble.

The last problem was the biggest in the end, from crossing the border to go in to the last soldier leaving we had a time limit of forty eight hours. This was a late addition to the restrictions to take some of the heat out of the UKs' domestic optics on this. After that apparently we would be viewed as an invading force and dealt with accordingly. That was the statement in parliament anyway, although I doubt if it had been run by the MoD prior to that to see if it was realistic. It might as well have been tweeted. The time thing. Jesus, from the first look at the whole thing, to do it right we would've needed at least seventy two hours in theory and probably more in practice. Now it was going to be rushed. Relying on speed will only carry the day so far...

In terms of our troops, technically it was all still Task Group Viking, in practice we had left people shoring up Donegal airport, there were still troops in the field properly cleaning out Donegal – we still hadn't assured ourselves that all the Carsonites had gone by that stage – we had people everywhere. We ended up with the TG Viking HQ, two of our own Companies, one reservist Company and holes filled by whomever 28 Bn could provide. As much soft skin transport as we could get was brought up to Finner and then we had a grand total of five Mowags. That was all that we could spare from 2 Cav. After all that fighting, look people forget that these things are just machines and they break down, especially if you keep shooting them with stuff. It wasn't much, but it was what we had. So the plan was, we would insert a Company plus the HQ by Chinook and the rest would drive in From Finner, through Beleek and along the A46 to Camp Erne. That bit went ok. Everything else went to shit the moment we stepped off the heli...'

On arriving at Camp Erne, Comdt Dave Heallys' A Coy, Task Group Viking were immediately struck by two things. One, there was many more people than initially planned for. Instead of the eight hundred they expected, the small camp was crowded with one thousand seven hundred and forty two men, women and children of all ages. The second was that the camp was in the middle of a major cornavirus outbreak, with as many as four hundred symptomatic 'active' cases being quarantined in a corner of the portacabin and tent based camp. Approximately eight hundred of the people there had been vaccinated, leaving five hundred people who had to be considered as having been exposed to the virus. With shared sanitation and feeding blocks, everyone had to be considered a close contact and simply tracing the indivuals a patient may have been close to was imposiible.

Doing the sums, each Chinook in a casevac role could only take twenty four stretchers, each AW139 could take four. These numbers reduced considerably when the patients needed critical care en route. Further complicating the issue was that these patients could not just be brought straight to an Irish hospital or refugee camp across the border – the numbers would simply overwhelm the existing facilities. The request for more time and helicopter movements was relayed up the line. The response was helicopter movements yes, time no. As the first elements of the ground convoy rolled into the camp, the first Chinooks were also landing to begin what became a non stop rolling medevac mission lasting until the end of the operation.

Comdt Brian Rafferty AC Ret'd

'We knew there'd be casualties that needed to go by air– IDP camps aren't exactly known world wide for conditions that produce athletes are they? So we were prepared for a certain amount of sick and injured, but when we were told to move four hundred active Covid-19 patients and another five hundred suspect cases to the Glen? Everyone knew that was impossible in the time we had. But, you know, we got to it and did as much as we could. It meant throwing everything we had at the task, the original plan went out the window, machines were pulled off maintenance where they could be put back together, crews were called in off rest, everything. At one stage, we had four Chinooks and six AW139s just shuttling people out.

Initially we took them to the Glen where our own new field hospital had been set up, and they were being packaged off by road and another two AW139s from there to hospitals around the country. This was too slow, but once the whole operation had been approved, the Germans had offered another field hospital and two CH 53 helicopters to move people. This was set up in Finner and with their helicopters now doing the shuttling within Ireland as well as our own, we actually managed to make quite a difference. We would land, load up stretchers, take them back to Finner, offload rotors running and then the Germans would move those that could be moved as quickly as possible to the Glen. After the first few runs, we were running out of stretchers so we kept the ones we had in the aircraft and just loaded people on bedsheets, roll mats – whatever they could be carried in. We actually moved the four hundred or so active cases quicker than we thought, some of them were effectively walking wounded.

After that, we had to pause, strip out the machines and sanitise them and then go back into get the suspect cases – we didn't want to start a new pandemic by bringing people who only might be normal sick into an infected environment. We were also running out of fuel in Finner itself – the fuel farm there had been expanded underground but all those helicopters go through a lot of juice. While that was being refilled by trucks coming up from Baldonnel, we also flew in fuel cells with one of the Chinooks, just to keep us going. We refitted all the helicopters with seats and we half expected things to speed up significantly. Civilians aren't troops though, and getting them loaded just seemed to take an age. In some cases helicopters would orbit overhead, waiting for space to land at the camp and then have to head back to Finner empty, just beacuse it took so long to get people organised and onto the machines. We got it done though, and even moved a few loads of the vacinated IDPs as well, so I think the ground troops only ended up having to move around five hundred in the end. But it kept going for the duration – the last heli left the camp at the same time as the trucks.'

Cpl Diane Keane

'For all the time we'd been at war, it sounds stupid now, but our focus had always been on protecting Ireland, stopping it all coming south. We nearly forgot, or it was put to the back of our mind what we were protecting the place from? We forgot that the people just up the road from us really were getting hammered worse than any unit in the DF. It was a real shock when we pulled into the camp that first morning. The PSNI guys meeting us, they looked like they were happy just to be handing over some of the burden around the place. They were holding it together pretty well under the circumstances, but you could see the strain on their faces. Young men and women looking older than their years. Maybe they thought the same about us.

Once you got inside the gate, the fence around the whole area was just a chicken wire fence, nothing fancy. It was just as much to mark the bounds of the place as any kind of security. Once you got inside. The people there, so many more than what we were expecting but the state they were in. You had to remember – they'd been driven from their homes in fear, so they didn't always have much with them. Think if your house was on fire, and you ran out without something as simple as your car keyes? How would you carry anything else? While people are shooting at you?

They were almost universally in a bad way in terms of just general exhaustion and stress, but I'll say something for the people running the place, they were still being properly fed and had safe running water. That on it's own saved lives. The sick though, the Covid-19 cases. The place was over full to start with, so the amount of Covid-19 cases just overwhelmed the care available. You had every stage there from mild cough to people dying on stretchers who needed an ICU. It was horrific to watch.

I saw some lads, lads who'd seen plenty of fighting and handled it as well as any of us could. They broke when they had to start moving these people, and the docs might take them to one side and say 'that one has to stay here'. Too sick to move, expectant. They weren't going to make the journey alive, they didn't have the equipment to hand to treat them and they would die if they were moved. So they died right there instead. And people who could make it went instead. I never saw that in combat, never mind to see it like this with just *normal people*... and that was the whole thing that really hit home to me then, during that operation. The whole time we had been fighting, your horizons are pretty close, you know? It's don't get killed today in the Sliabh Blooms, or make it to the end of the night in Donegal, or just don't put your foot down on the next step without looking that there's no IED in front of you. Nothern Ireland itself became an abstract thing, a far away place; even when we were looking at it right in front of us. But in reality it's just people. That could have been anyones' families that we were dealing with there. There's no difference.'

While the bulk of the deployed soldiers secured the immediate area, organised the landing sites, moved people by road and generally tried to smooth the flow of people out of the camp, other organisations were not resting. The second day of the operation was to be a bitter one.

On the back of a report from an outbound Chinook that several roadblocks were being formed on the A46, blocking the fastest route back to Finner, the company of reservists and members of 28 Bn who now formed C Coy of Task Group Viking began to patrol the hills and roads back towards the sighting. A company strength patrol was stretching the terms of the agreement on how they could operate while still within Northern Ireland, but was considered an necessary evil under the circumstances. Once again, moving in such a large formation was providing mixed results among the reservists whose competence and comfort zone lay strictly in small unit warfare.

Approaching the roadblock and lead by a Mowag, with dismounted soldiers flanking in the fields on either side, the patrol stopped, not wanting to drive into what was very likely a booby trapped obstacle. As the soldiers moved forward they came under sniper fire from the far side of the roadblock. Returning fire, the patrol withdrew.

There was neither the time nor the authority to follow through on the attack under the circumstances. Had they done so, they would have found that the series of roadblocks – tractors, buses and other vehicles overturned on the road – were indeed mined. They would also have found that they were under fire not from

Carsonites but from Dissidents,who regarded any victory over Carsonites, PSNI or Irish Defence Forces all to be equally a success. As the morning of this second day ran into afternoon and the patrol returned to Camp Erne, the A46 had to be given up as closed, and a new route out was planned along the Glenasheevar Road. Robbing from the title of a Bernard Fall book, this became known as An Sráid Gan Áthas – Irelands very own Street Without joy.

Comdt Dave Heally

' We'd sent off as many as we could by air, but the clock was really ticking now, you know? Politically... We were all aware of the tensions but no one knew what was meant by 'treated as an invading force' specifically, but it wasn't going to be good was it? We'd given up on the A46, ostensibly the fastest way out, due to the time pressure. We could have forced through the roadblocks and the inevitable ambushes there but it would've taken too much time. So, we'd already sent out quite a few of the soft skin vehicles in the opposite direction towards Enniskillen and then down the N4 – the goal at that stage was just 'get across the border', it was all people without Covid-19 onboard at that point so it wasn't as critical to get to a camp or a hospital, just to get out of the North. We thought... no, we'd hoped that the forces that had been laying roadblocks and sniping that morning was all there was, that that was the big play they were making?

It wasn't entirely unreasonable, we knew we'd given them a serious bloody nose over the last while so maybe they hadn't gotten as organised as the int had claimed? Talk about indulging in wishful thinking. Maybe we thought that way because we didn't have a choice. The only way out for the last troops and refugees by that evening was to exit back towards the west along the Glenasheevar Road to Lough Melvin, cross the border towards Rossinver then hang a right along the southern shore of the lake and then leisurely drive back into Finner, being at that point able to give the proper attention to convoy security etc etc.

But the time was really against us, only a few hours. I know, anyone looking back at this is saying no route recce, not enough flank security all that and I know. We didn't have enough of what we needed, B Coy had escorted the previous soft skins out of the area with two of the Mowags, so we had three plus enough trucks for us – A Coy and C Coy. Our Task Group HQ had gone out to Finner with the last helicopters to start getting set up there for our arrival and we expected follow on taks too. It had just been that kind of month, so it was fair enough for them wanting to get ahead of that. My orders then, as the senior Comdt left, was to oversee the move out.

The Glenasheevar road for those who aren't familiar with it, runs east – west pretty much, from Lough Erne Lower where the IDP camp was to Lough Melvin which is itself split down the middle by the border. For most of that route, it goes through a shallow valley with hills on either side. It's more or less single track all the way for the size of vehicles we had. Left and right, you had roads lined by trees, you had farmland, few enough houses but they were there... Look, someone reading this with hindsight is saying 'you drove down a one lane road, overlooked on both sides with ample cover for the enemy?'. We weren't blind to that at the time, trust me – I was already worried. But the only threat we'd encountered had been on the A46, the northern side of the hills. And, once again, time was the main thing we were worried about.

So the plan was, when you can't use the kind of normal, careful process that you'd like but you have to do something anyway, what do you do? You do it fast. That was the plan. Two Mowags up front, one at the rear, trucks in the middle and get down that road as fast as possible. We'd briefed of course on what to do in the event of roadblocks or ambushes. We planned that any time we stopped, we'd put out flank security to recce the area. Technically we weren't allowed to do any of that, but we chose to interpret that as basic convoy security rather than 'carrying out any operations not linked to the humanitarian effort.' And then off we went.

We didn't know then, before leaving the IDP camp, that the sniping and roadblocks earlier had been from a small Dissident group that had been themselves following the Carsonites into the area, but hadn't been strong enough in numbers to engage them. The Carsonites themselves had infiltrated the high ground with about one hundred and fifty or so fighters, but crucially, they'd brought almost all of their heavy weapons – machine guns, RPGs and whatever few mortars they had left. I'm not sure if they had planned to engage so many of us, but they must have made the decison; correctly, that we would be hamstrung by trying to protect the civilians. We got about half way through the hills... '

Cpl Diane Keane

'We'd been on the road for about an hour and a half by this point – if you were driving a car on your own, you'd be there by now, but a convoy of three APCs and a two dozen trucks on small roads... everything takes longer. We had ourselves plus about three hundred civilians. Every time a car came the other way, we'd end up stopping. Every time we stopped, we'd deploy security. Get the car out of the way, then you had to get security on board again. We probably should have pinged it when the cars stopped coming that they were being stopped further down the road by something else. I was in one of the trucks about half way back down the convoy, so alot of what I was getting in terms of knowing what was going on was just listening to the radio, or when we dismounted to do security.

Big picture? What happened was that the Carsonites had gotten into the hills and taken a gamble that we'd go this way rather than force the roadblocks the nationalists had put in on the main road – they could listen to the news as well as anyone and knew the restrictions we had. Little picture? They just picked a good spot for an ambush and set themselves up.

We were at a spot where we had ground rising on the right of the convoy – the northern side – and pretty flat to the left with ditches on both sides of the road so that manouvering would be difficult. They dug themselves in on a long, well ridge would be too much of a word, but basically where the line of the incline on the right went flat and met the horizon. Apparently, the trigger of the whole event was a tractor stopped at an angle across the road, no driver. That was what had turned around any other cars coming down, although undoubtedly some of those cars were Carsonites checking our progress, how long the convoy was, that kind of thing.

The first Mowag stopped well back from the tractor and that I think saved a lot of lives. There was a minute where nothing was happening, the majority of C Coy were put out on the right and a Platoon of A Coy went in the ditch on the left because you could already see everything that way. Looking back now, I'd say, maybe the Carsonites were having a 'what do we do now?' moment. C Coy got about half way up the field, the front vehicles were still well back from the obstacle and then it just all... it all happened very quickly.

The plan obviously, had been to hit our first and last vehicles, trap us in. They'd stuffed rocket warheads in the tractor and more a few hundred metres back where they expected the last APC to be. When they decided to go with it, the tractor exploded and fragged a few of our own, but apart from the shock, the Mowag and crew were alright. That second explosion though, the one that was supposed to be at the back? That was buried in the ditch on our right and hit one of the trucks a few vehicles back from us. It just disappeared in flash and was gone. The vehicles either side got it pretty bad and were effectively disabled, the cab of the one behind took the worst of it for them, but the one in front... They were all killed, soldiers and civilians alike, thirty people gone just like that. There were another fifteen in the one that was, I don't know the right word for it, atomised I suppose.

Look, I'm describing this one after another, but it all happened at once, okay? When the IEDs went off, they also opened up with machine guns and RPGs. The just swept the whole line of vehicles. The tarp on the side of ours, you could hear it making that noise it makes when you hit a taught plastic like that, like a ripping and ticking noise at that same time.

With the bombs going off, I froze for a second, but when the bullets started hitting the sides, we hit the bed of the truck first and then all piled out the tail gate when it became apparent the truck wasn't moving anywhere – we weren't driving through the ambush. Four died in that truck and six more were injured. Tom McIntyre, Pte Tom McIntyre was one of the dead. First burst of fire through the side of the truck , he was hit in the back and neck, dead instantly. The others were civilians that stood up in panic to get out. We rolled out the back and into the ditch on the right. That was the first chance I had to look around me, really. That scene was grim. There at least four more trucks burning from RPG hits and mortars were landing in the field just behind us, as much to keep us in place as anything else, but it was the machine guns that were doing the damage. You could hear the rounds snapping overhead and see the little, barely visible, trails of smoke if an RPG went overhead. Being honest, I wasn't even paying attention to the mortars by then.They seemed like a 'I'll deal with that later' kind of problem.

From where we were, we couldn't fire back because C Coy were in the line of fire, half way up the hill and really, they looked to be all either pinned down or dead by that point. We were there , I don't know, it can't have been long but there was obviously a minute where we didn't have control of things. Then the Mowag at the rear of the convoy opened up. They'd gotten over the ditch on the right and were in the field on that side firing their .50 calibre machine gun into the line of enemy. At that point, some semblance of command and control came back online. The convoy was split behind, we couldn't get forward with any speed because of the remains of the tractor and a sizable crater. So what do you do? You attack.

To my front, there was the remains of a stone wall that might give us some cover, so I moved my guys up behind that. The Mowag was drawing some of the fire, but there was still plenty for everyone so we were staying low. It finally gave us an angle where we could fire without hitting C Coy. It was only fleeting shots we were getting in before another nest would open up, but we started to get effective fire down on them after a while. It was from there that I actually looked back properly for the first time, still lying down behind this crappy broken wall only one stone high by then. What I saw. There's that picture that ended up in the media that, well it's going to be the one that is always used when people talk about this, isn't it. What I saw was just like that. The lines of trucks, one Mowag burning at the front by that time, and the other trying to manuevre around it under fire... And the bodies. The piles of bodies at the backs of the trucks, everyone all mixed together... That's just one of those snapshots in your brain that's there forever.'

Still, it is unclear who initially ordered C Coy to advance into the withering fire of the ambush. Most likely, they are dead themselves or have chosen to remain silent. What is clear, is that when the company comprised of reservists and regulars, entered the field on the northern side of the ambush site,there were one hundred and twenty two men and women amongst them. When they reached the firing line at the top of the incline following their mad dash up the middle of the ambush, protected only by a few smoke grenades, there were fewer than fifty remaining. By the time they swept through the nearest positions with a rage, there was only forty one people left unharmed.

Of the remaining eighty one, forty seven were dead and the rest wounded. Holding the nearest Carsonite fighters under fire allowed the remains of A Coy and the two APCs to close in and either destroy or put to flight the remaing enemy fighters. Still located in Northern Ireland, there was no prospect of further pursuit. Even if Task Group Viking was of a mind to continue the fight, they had more pressing issues. The Butchers Bill for the ambush on Glenasheevar Road was, in total eighty four dead Irish soldiers and one hundred and sixteen dead civilans – the IDPs they had been there to rescue. The scale of the ambush meant that there was some relenting on the restrictions and further troops from 28 Bn and 2 Cav were allowed to enter the area to help extract the wounded, dead and surviving members of Task Group Viking. One of the darkest days in modern Irish military history, it would also mark the last large combat action of the war.

CONCLUSION

Time to reflect in both combat and politics is often lacking. Usually, when it comes, it has come at great price. The short time surrounding the events from the first Carsonite push into Donegal to the battered survivors of TG Viking returning to Finner were a period of great political tension and friction, bookended by these brutal actions. It offered a moment of tragedy around which people could gather and put aside, or at very least moderate their differences. French, Irish and UK forces had come close to accidentally clashing in the skies. Irish troops, backed by the EU had made an incursion into Northern Ireland under condition that almost assured catastrophe, the risk of which was only accepted for humanitarian reasons.

Severely reduced in number, the Carsonites and Dissidents both returned to a lessor phase of warfare. Not without death, this level of conflict has been deemed 'background' by some commentators in an almost word for word recital of Russian doctrine in the area, escalate to de-escalate. As for the Russians, it does appear that their goals were met. The EU and UK were both damaged politically by several years of warfare on their own turf. This, presumably, was the idea all along. Cause damage, reduce an enemys strength, provide yourself room to move in some other political, economic or military arena. Post Covid-19, they have enjoyed more political space to recover than their distracted competitors. In this, Ireland, North and South was just their chosen battlefield.

It does *appear* that large scale arms shipments have stopped. The intelligence picture does seem to indicate that Russia too was surprised by the attack into Donegal. Moreover, for the numbers of Dissident and Carsonite fighters remaining, there are ample weapons left for a lower level of conflict to continue for some time. This too may suit the Russian agenda over time.

Severely reduced from their peak strength, the various paramilitary groupings are no longer considered capable of mounting any kind of large scale action. Shunned by their own communities for the pain they have caused, the continue to operate outside of society. As already mentioned however, a level of violence continues, mostly directed at each other. Without any significant number of replacements being willing to join them, it seems possible they will simply attrite each other out of existance. They could simply cease and disband of course, but it is most likely that too many personal rubicons have been crossed. These people cannot go home in their own country, they cannot assume that their enemy will simply stop, because they themselves will not stop. So what do they have left then? Perhaps they will simply wait, expecting always the sound of footsteps behind them, or helicopters muffled by terrain, coming closer.

Of those who have graciously allowed me to use their interviews here, and to be identifed, it seems only right to 'wrap up' their stories to date.

Senator Ian Davis resigned as Minister for Defence six weeks after the operation to rescue IDPs in Northern Ireland. This was not in reaction to the ambush itself, but to the intelligence picture that was emerging almost immediately in it's aftermath – the major threat to the state was ending. The processes he had put in place to replace and reinforce the Defence Forces were working with a lesser but still acceptable flow of new entrants. To his mind, the culture in the Department of Defence had been sufficently changed as to insure that the policies put in place would continue, unless a serious change of national circumstances dictate otherwise. He has returned to his retirement, full time.

Comdt Dave Heally suffered serious burn and shrapnel wounds from a rocket propelled grenade in the first volley fired at the convoy on Glenasheevar road. This injury and those of the command element around him accounted for the delay in decisive action on the day. In support of those who did take over, he will tell you that the circumstances meant he couldn't have done any better anyway. Still recovering from his injuries, he is currently on a Command and Staff Course in the DF Training Centre in the Curragh. He has already been told he will be filling a Lt Col position in Ops in DFHQ when he completes his studies.

Comdt Brian Rafferty left the Air Corps for a job in the resurgent civil sector, seeking a more regular work life balance for his family. Ominously, the retention problem suffered by the Air Corps began to emerge again as soon as the post Covid-19 travel environement returned to normal, and the airlines were hiring again. Comdt Raferty however has eschewed the airlines for a career in search and rescue and is currently flying with a company based in Cyprus.

'Brendan', the one Red Team member who spoke to me has remained with the unit as it has regularised into what is now officially called the Defence Forces Opposition Forces Cell. It is still called the Red Team by everyone else. When asked what his job currently involves, he simply replied 'Keeping busy'.

Sgt Andy Cunningham is currently overseas in the Golan Heights area of Syria.

Cpl Diane Keane is currently on her Standard NCOs course for promotion to Sgt. She was awarded a Distinguished Service Medal for her actions on the Glenasheevar Road, having been the first Section Commander to lead her troops forward to flank the enemy firing line. She herself has somewhat downplayed her contribution when compared to other accounts. The troops of her section on the day credit her with keeping them alive and enagaging the enemy effectively. Of note, she recounts that her mother Valerie has returned ro work, but is still feeling the longterm effects of her illness with Covid-19 19. When asked what she is doing now, Diane was vague but mentioned 'training'. From other snippets of conversation, I believe she has also joined the Red Team in some capacity.

The new Ptes regarded Cpl Lucasz McGrath during the patrol brief with a look he was becoming accustomed to in the last six months. That 'wanting to ask, but afraid of the answer' look that he got from anyone who hadn't been on the Glenasheevar Road. The eyes said, 'what was it like to be under fire? How did you make it to the top? What did you do when you got there...' Unconsciously below even those enquiries, was the one they asked of themselves 'could I do the same?'.

Getting ready to head out in a small patrol in Co Monaghan, he knew Jan Nowak was getting the same silent interrogation in the other briefing room. He returned the stare of the nervous, fresh out of training reservists, absorbing their unasked questions for a moment. Had they spoke them aloud, he thought, how would he answer them; except to say that with luck, they would never find out.

In writing this book, I was putting down on paper a couple of ideas that had been floating around in my head and trying to make them somewhat coherent.

These ideas originated when I was told, while still serving in the Irish Air Corps, that I would be putting together a new block of lectures for the air power module of the Command and Staff course in the Defence Forces Training School. This is the course required for Commandants in the Defence Forces to advance to Lieutenant Colonel, it lasts for about ten months and is fairly intense. To put it in perspective, students are required to complete a civilian Masters while also doing full days and nights of purely military studies. Faced with that, I left the Air Corps. The End.

Just kidding. A block of lectures on such a technical subject runs the risk of hitting the death by powerpoint mark very quickly. You put endless streams of information on the screen and watch everyones eyes roll in their heads. To get around that, I decided I would try to go for scenario based lecturing - create a series of ever escalating events that needed airpower support and say to the students 'How do you plan that operation?' At least it would be more interesting.

Nevertheless, I did actually leave the Air Corps before I had to do any of that, but the ideas still bounced around a bit and changed shape. Looking around at some of the public conversation on Brexit and the Defence Forces in general, I decided why not? If there's a message in the book at all, it's that any future Brexit outcome should also include a real and critical assesment of what it means for Irelands ability to provide for the publics security. Like it or not, it's a real thing that requires investment and attention on an ongoing basis.

My apologies to more or less everyone in Northern Ireland, which is reduced mostly to background noise in the book, despite being where most of the actual impact of a conflict would be felt. I was trying to not give the characters or the narrator any more insight or knowledge than they would actually have and this precluded a more diverse set of voices.

Finally, if you liked the book, please leave a review on Amazon or Goodreader, tweet about it or just recommend it to someone else. For independantly published books like, that's how they get read and your help is graciously received.

Declan Daly
Sept 2020

Medevac: Flying The Irish Air Corps' Hems Mission

Commandant Declan Daly (Ret'd)

Author's note:

The whole idea behind properly writing down my experience of flying on EAS came after talking to Corporal Mick Whelan, who was collecting recordings for the DF Oral History project. This records the experiences of individual members of the Defence Forces, of all ranks and roles, so that future historians will have something to go on that is more colourful, insightful and powerful than mere official records. I write some of those official records and it would be fair to say they are somewhat stripped of the human touch. The beauty of the oral history collection is that the Airman's story is just as important as the General's. It gives, or will give, a researcher a chance to cross reference the many lived experiences of an event or service against the more staid official records and thus allow a history of our time to be more nuanced and informed. It also gives the serviceman or woman their own voice on the topic – no one will have to guess or interpret what you were thinking if you tell them yourself. For any Defence Forces service member, of any rank, that hasn't taken the chance to give an interview to the project, I can only recommend that you do. It's not only worthwhile for the project, it's a very interesting thing to do for yourself and makes your story part of the history.

When I interviewed with Mick, I talked at length about EAS

amongst other parts of my service ,but came away feeling a bit frustrated as if I'd only scratched the surface. I was also struck that what I considered entirely normal, were things that other people might see as the most interesting part of a story. As a pilot, I would be taken in by the technical aspects, whereas Mick would come back to a topic frequently and ask 'How did you feel about that?" As a result, I've tried to include a bit of that side of things here, and tried to be a bit more expansive than 'I felt like I was at low level in bad weather'.

Any reader will notice that the people essentially missing from what I've written here are the patients themselves. The reason for this is down to patient confidentiality. We come across people on what may be the worst, or even last, day of their lives and I don't think it would be fair of me if I capitalised on that. I've tried as much as I can here to de- identify peoples' flights with us as much as I can (if you think a story about a patient with heart trouble going into Galway is about you, it's probably not I'm afraid, I've flown hundreds of those tasks and the service has flown thousands). There is one glaring exception to this and although no names are mentioned, I hope the families involved can accept that I have included that particular story to show how some tasks can cut through all the personal defences you may build up. Patient confidentiality also explains why some of the more 'spectacular' cases are not included here – it's not that they weren't noteworthy, it's just that one or two key descriptors on those jobs would certainly put that patient's identity in no doubt.

This is all very much my own experience of EAS. I have tried to explain everyone else's role and any mistakes or oversimplifications there are mine alone. For any of my colleagues that find themselves reading this, if your name isn't mentioned, it's probably because the statute of limitations hasn't run out yet.

Glossary Of Barely Intelligible Aeromedical Helicopter Speak

EAS brings together people who are military helicopter techs, flying crews and national Ambulance Service clinical crews. These groups share several things in common, a dark humour that is made much worse and more inappropriate by exposure to each other (think Grim Reaper drawing a dead soul with a human bone, on a canvas of black holes, that kind of dark), and a language that is usually considered incomprehensible to those who don't work with us regularly.

Look, to be honest, sometimes we're just making up words to sound smart in front of other people, but most of the time, this language forms a verbal shorthand that saves us from having to expand on a concept or situation when time is of the essence. I don't want this to be a technically driven account, so I've tried to minimise the use of EAS jargon as much as I can, but in some places, it has to be used to give any context at all. To make things intelligible, here's some of the main offending items explained, the rest should hopefully become clear from the main text:

Cyclic : The stick in front of the pilot that controls pitch and roll. Stick goes forward houses get bigger, stick goes back, houses get smaller. Left and right just roll you left and right.

Collective : The handbrake looking thing on the pilots left. This controls the pitch of the blades in the main rotor system (that's the one over your head) and also demands the right amount of power from the engines to keep those blades turning at the right speed. In the hover it will make you go vertically up and down. In forward flight, pulling it up means faster, down means slower.

Tail rotor control pedals : Also called anti-torque pedals. These control the tail rotor and move the aircraft around in the yaw plane, see further below to find out what that is. They are also used to counter the torque produced by the main gearbox when you dump two jet turbine engines worth of power into it.

POF: Principles of flight, the aerodynamic and mathematical principles that make a helicopter get off the ground. Heli POF is considered by many of our other aviation colleagues to be some kind of dark magic, so we just tell them we sacrifice a chicken on the nose of the aircraft first thing in the morning and, if the omens are good, we go flying.

ETL: Effective Translational Lift. When you move from a hover to forward flight (or any other direction actually) you pass through a speed where you gain effective translational lift. This is the bit where you stop 'hovering' and start 'flying'. At this point you can kind of think of the rotor blades as forming a disk that kind of works like an airplanes wing. Why 'kind of'? Because there's a lot more going on than that, but just go with it for now. The main point of it all for the pilot, is that you require less engine power above ETL (up to a certain speed), than you do in a hover. If you are doing a recce at high weights, down wind and drop below ETL without realizing it, you may find yourself running out of the engine power required to stay at whatever altitude you're at. This is a bad thing.

LTE: Loss of Tail Rotor Effect. Nothing has broken but for whatever reason, you've asked for more directional control than your tail rotor can give. Can mainly happen if you're heavy, if you're down wind with no airspeed or from a combination of a number of other things that you should really have avoided in the first place. It will manifest itself by you running out of travel on the yaw pedals and the aircraft starting to rotate. You get out of it easy enough by putting the nose down for speed and letting off a bit of power (and thus torque), but both of these require altitude. Thankfully, not a big issue for the AW139 unless you really ask for it, but I've seen it on Garda Air Support Unit (GASU) EC135s which tend to be well loaded up at all times.

Wx: Weather (warning: Met Forecasters should look away now – this is a massively gross oversimplification). Ireland sits at the same latitude as parts of Alaska but we usually avoid some of their colder conditions. The reason is that Ireland is situated on the edge of the Atlantic where most of our weather systems originate. It's also where the Gulf Stream, which brings warmer water up from around Mexico approaches landfall. This warmer water evaporates and moves inland. This means that we have a largely temperate climate that is influenced by the ocean but with a warm bit providing greater amounts of rainfall. We also have winds coming across the ocean uninterrupted and hitting our West Coast, which gives us our sometimes sprightly breezes. Compounding this, as you move inland, the country is more or less flat in the middle but filled with rivers, lakes and bogs which provide ample extra moisture to provide fog when conditions are right.

During Winter time, instead of temperate Atlantic weather, we will often get cold Northerly winds coming down from Siberia bringing polar air masses. If cold enough, these bring freezing temperatures but clear skies.

Predicting weather in Ireland can't be easy as it's frequently different every thirty nautical miles or so. The critical margins for us as heli crews, from about 5KM vis down and cloudbases of about 500 feet or less, can be so massively affected by local conditions that you just have to accept sometimes that you will have 10KM vis or none at all and be prepared to work accordingly.

Yaw plane: How to explain, if you were to look at a helicopter from above and observe how it runs left or right, flat, the same way a car would, that's the yaw plane.

Vis: Visibility – the distance in meters that you can see and positively identify an object. Positively is the key word – if you can see a glowing ball of light in the mist where a town should be 5KM away, you do not have 5KM vis. If you can see a windfarm on a clear day 20Km away, you have 10+ vis because that's what will be written down in a weather report.

TAF: Terminal Area Forecast – The weather forecast for an airport for a given period of time. There are Short TAFS (likely to be somewhat accurate for VFR flight) and Long TAFS (likely to be fictional the longer you go from when they were issued).

VFR: Visual Flight Rules – you are flying and navigating by reference to what you can see outside the window. There are minimum limits for launch for VFR flight rules, in our case 3Km vis and 500'. This will seem high to some other operators, but they are there because if you launch on 3 Km and 500 feet in Ireland, you won't go far without finding No KM and No hundred feet.

Met Eireann: The national agency that provides weather forecasts and other acts of wizardry. Whilst they are certainly practitioners of dark arts, I've found them to be generally a nice bunch of people, doing their best to give us the best information possible.

IFR: Instrument Flight Rules – Flying by reference to your cockpit instruments and, in normal operations, largely reliant on your destination being equipped with a standard of navigation aides high enough to allow you to land. This almost exclusively means airports.

VOR: VHF Omnidirectional Radio – a ground based nav aide that sends out signals like spokes on a wheel. Each spoke is called a radial and can be used to indicate where you are in relation to an airport.

ILS : Instrument Landing System – Two sets of radio equipment that send out very narrow beam signals in a cone expanding outward from source. When you are in the middle of each cone, you know you are lined up laterally and vertically on your chosen runway.

DME: Distance Measuring Equipment – Another nav aid that tells you how far away from it you are. Used in conjunction with ILS and VORs to make up an instrument approach.

Approach Chart : Or Jeppesen Chart, or just Jeppe Chart .This is a page that gives a written and pictorial set of instructions to a crew working under IFR on how to land at a given runway without flying into the surrounding countryside or other aircraft.

Task: A task, call, shout or job is a request from the NACC for us to go on a specific mission to pick up a patient or treat them at scene for onward transport by an ambulance.

NACC: National Aeromedical Control Centre. A one-person desk based in the ambulance control centre in Tallaght that must be manned 24/7 and tasks all aeromedical flights, be they EAS, fixed wing international transport or other rotary wing domestic or international flights.

CFIT: Controlled Flight into Terrain – Crashing an otherwise serviceable aircraft for anyone of about twenty billion reasons. Still happens occasionally despite all the barriers we try to put in place and all the technology we throw at helicopters to stop it.

Deconfliction: Making sure you're not in the same bit of sky as another aircraft at the same time. Depending on the type of airspace you are working in, deconfliction will either be provided by ATC, or by mutual agreement over the radio. If all else fails, look out the window and don't fly into other aircraft.

ICAO: International Civil Aviation Organisiation – the body that sets out the standards that must be met worldwide by national or regional regulators. ICAO Annex 14 for example, sets out what criteria are needed to actually call something a heli-pad including safe approach angles, distances from obstacles and the size of the actual concrete circle on the ground.

Challenge and Response: The normal way of completing a checklist in a multicrew aircraft, not a duel to the death. For example, the Challenge by one pilot during the Pre-Start checks could be 'Circuit Breakers'. The Response by the other pilot will be to physically and visually check the CB panels and call 'all in'.

DPKO Aviation Manual: The UN Department of Peace Keeping Operations Aviation Manual. Basically, this is how to do aviation the UN way. Coming from a military background the UN way was incredibly frustrating and inefficient.

Welcome To Eas

Up front in the cockpit, it's Paul's first day as a fully minted EAS Co-Pilot (P2). In the back, Luke is on his first shadow shift – flying as an observer, learning from the more experienced crew-members before going live on his own as an EAS crewman/EMT. Myself, Jamie- our crewman and Pat - our Advanced Paramedic (AP) have been doing this for a while.

The first task we receive from the NACC dispatcher is a good 'first job' for the newer guys. It's a pick-up of a patient with a suspected STEMI in Tobercurry, North of Knock Airport. The weather is a stable cloud base at 600 – 700 feet with 10+ vis underneath. There's enough involved that the newer guys will have to do a bit of thinking about our route, but no real pressure on the rest of us so we can help the learning process along as much as possible. Everything goes fine on the outbound leg, the weather stays unusually 'the same' and even with the pick-up site on rising ground, the cloud doesn't touch the ground until about a mile North of our target.

It stays this way until we land on at Galway Hospital. I notice a flurry of activity in the back and Pat calls 'Cab off' – he wants to isolate the comms in the back from the cockpit. I look over my shoulder and see Luke starting chest compressions on the previously stable patient who has gone into cardiac arrest just as we touched down. As this is Paul's first real job, I decide to keep this to myself and we run through the shutdown checks as normal in the cockpit – you never know how people will react the first time this happens around them and it's usually quickest and safest to just get things done like you always would. By the time the engines wind down enough to hear what's happening in the back, the patient is alive again and moaning at Luke to stop hurting her chest. This is all normal; the lads take it perfectly in their stride. A fairly standard 'Welcome to EAS'.

Introduction

Since 1963, the Irish Air Corps has provided an unbroken service to the state in terms of moving the sick and injured around the country by helicopter. Starting with the Alouette III, the Air Corps introduced an air ambulance service moving patients in need of specialist care from regional hospitals to major ones where definitive care was available. The Air Corps also introduced Ireland's first Search and Rescue (SAR) capability, but although there's an overlap in the end result to the patient, this is a very different service. Through the years, various different aircraft have been used to move patients between hospitals, with the advent of the Dauphin helicopter allowing a comparatively limited night time capability. These were all however hospital to hospital or hospital to airport missions, today they would be described as an IHT (Inter Hospital Transfer) or Tertiary HEMS. This means that patients were not being moved from the scene of an incident to hospital. In 2011, the Air Corps began a pilot project in concert with the National Ambulance Service to assess the need for a national HEMS. Initially envisaged as a one-year assessment, this mission began flying in 2012 and became what we today call the Emergency Aeromedical Service. Despite responding to thousands of calls in the intervening years, not much is publicly advertised about how we go about our business or what is involved for a crewmember who wants to fly a HEMS mission in Ireland. Having been fortunate enough to be involved from the very beginning of the service, this is my own experience of flying HEMS in Ireland.

Medevac : Flying The Irish Air Corps HEMS Mission is availble on Amazon

Made in the USA
Middletown, DE
25 June 2021

43152574R00113